ONE-EYED CAT

YEARLING BOOKS/YOUNG YEARLINGS/YEARLING CLASSICS are designed especially to entertain and enlighten young people. Patricia Reilly Giff, consultant to this series, received her bachelor's degree from Marymount College and a master's degree in history from St. John's University. She holds a Professional Diploma in Reading and a Doctorate of Humane Letters from Hofstra University. She was a teacher and reading consultant for many years, and is the author of numerous books for young readers.

ONE–EYED CAT

Paula Fox

A LITTLE YEARLING BOOK

Published by
Dell Publishing
a division of
Bantam Doubleday Dell Publishing Group, Inc.
1540 Broadway
New York, New York 10036

The trademark Yearling® is registered in the U.S. Patent and Trademark Office.

The trademark Dell® is registered in the U.S. Patent and Trademark Office.

ISBN: 0-440-76641-9

Reprinted by arrangement with Bradbury Press, an affiliate of Macmillan, Inc.

Printed in the United States of America

June 1993

10 9 8 7 6

RAD

For my sons
GABRIEL and ADAM
and for my brothers
JAMES and KEITH

CONTENTS

There was a child went forth every day,
And the first object he look'd upon, that object he became,
And that object became part of him for the day or a
    certain part of the day,
Or for many years or stretching cycle of years.

—WALT WHITMAN

I

Sunday

NED WALLIS WAS THE MINISTER'S ONLY CHILD. THE Congregational Church where the Reverend James Wallis preached stood on a low hill above a country lane a mile beyond the village of Tyler, New York. Close by the parsonage, a hundred yards or so from the church, was a small cemetery of weathered tombstones. Some had fallen over and moss and ivy covered them. When Ned first learned to walk, the cemetery was his favorite place to practice. There, his father would come to get him after the members of the congregation had gone home to their Sunday dinners. There, too, his mother often sat on a tumbled stone and watched over him while his father stood at the great church door speaking to each and every person who had attended service that day. That was long ago, before his mother had become ill.

1

Just past the church was a low, dark, musty-smelling barn where people had stabled their horses in the days before there were automobiles. In bad weather, it was still used by ancient Mr. Deems, who drove his rattling buckboard and skinny chestnut mare all the way from his farm in the valley to the church and into the barn. And when Ned grew older, he and a few of the children from the early Sunday school class played there, hiding and shouting and scaring each other but keeping their distance from Mr. Deems's mare, who was known to be cross tempered. On warm days the voices of the choir—especially the high tremulous voices of the oldest singers—would float into the darkness of the barn like the thin, sweet aroma of meadow flowers. The children would pause in their play and listen until old Mrs. Brewster, who held the last note of a hymn till her breath ran out and she tottered into her seat, fell silent.

The Wallis family didn't live in the parsonage, although they could have and it would not have cost them a penny. Their house was fifteen miles from Tyler. It had been built by Ned's grandfather in 1846, nearly eighty years before Ned was born. Like the church, it stood on a hill. From its windows there was a view of the Hudson River. This view was one of the reasons the Reverend Wallis did not want to move.

It was a big, ailing old house. When things went wrong with it—the furnace cut o it wasn't supposed to, the cistern overflowed, th roof leaked—or when Ned's mother's illness grew worse so that Reverend Wallis could hardly bear to leave her to take care of his many pastoral duties, then he would cry out that they would have to go and live in the parsonage, such a mean, small house, so far from the heart-lifting sight of the great river. Ned knew that his father loved the house that was such a trouble to take care of, too far from his church, too costly for a country minister's salary.

When Ned followed his father into the church on Sundays, he was always startled by the vast airy openness above the aisles and rows of pews, and by the immense height of the windows which flowed with light, and by the many dark gold-colored pipes of the organ which rose behind the pulpit. No matter how often he counted them, he always ended up with a different number. He knew every part of the church, from the cellar where the huge furnace glowed in cold weather like a steam locomotive, to the basement where the Sunday school classes and meetings and study clubs were held, and on special occasions, where church suppers were spread out on long tables, all the way up the curving narrow steps to the gallery above the choir. Perhaps he was always surprised by the bigness of the church because he was used to thinking of it as another room in his house.

One Sunday in late September, a few days before his eleventh birthday, Ned was leaning back in the front pew where he usually sat. The red velvet pew cushion, so comforting in winter, was making the backs of his legs itch. The August heat had held on and the sky was pale with it. Papa's voice, as he preached his sermon, seemed to come from a great distance. Someone coughed. Someone else rustled the pages of a hymnbook. A cloud of drowsiness dropped over Ned like a cloth. He tried to keep himself awake by imagining what it would be like to live on the ocean for all of your life. That was what had happened to Philip Nolan in *The Man Without a Country*: he had been exiled to a ship. Ned had just finished the book that morning before he went downstairs to have breakfast with Papa. The thought of breakfast woke Ned up completely. It reminded him of Mrs. Scallop.

Until two months ago, Sunday breakfasts had been quiet. Ned's Papa always wore his amethyst tiepin in his black silk tie, his black trousers with the satin stripe down each side and the cutaway jacket with back panels that looked like a beetle's folded wings, and he had his Sunday look, thinking about his sermon, Ned knew. The only noise had been their spoons hitting the sides of the cereal bowls. Sometimes Ned would gaze up at the Tiffany-glass lamp shade with its various panels depicting wild animals. Ned's favorite was the camel who stood in a brown glass desert which appeared to stretch for miles when the light was turned on. But that quietness had been shattered by the coming of Mrs. Scallop, whose voice now intruded in the dining room every morning, as sharp and grinding as the woodcutter's saw when he came in the spring to thin out the pines which grew along the north side of the Wallises' property.

Mrs. Scallop was the third housekeeper they had had in a year, and in Ned's opinion, the worst. She would stand at the table talking to them, her hands resting on her stomach. She didn't need questions or answers or any kind of conversation at all to keep going. Ned noticed how Papa's brow grew furrowed with lines, though he was as polite and kindly to Mrs. Scallop as he was to everyone else. On their way to church that morning in the old Packard car, Ned had said, "Mrs. Scallop talks to our chairs when we're not there."

Papa said, "She's very good to your mother. Poor woman. She's had a hard life—losing her husband only a year after they were married and having to support herself all these years."

Ned knew he would say something like that. But

5

earlier, when he'd told his mother his joke about Mrs. Scallop speaking to furniture, she'd laughed and told him Mrs. Scallop was frightened of groans and whispers. "If I whisper, 'Leave the napkin on the tray,' Mrs. Scallop disappears instantly," she said. Ned had started to smile. Then he couldn't—he'd thought of his mother's illness, which was rheumatoid arthritis, and how it really did make her groan, or so weak she could only whisper.

What puzzled Ned most about Mrs. Scallop were her sudden unexplained silences. They were far worse than her talking; they were angry silences, and the anger was even in her hands which she pressed so hard against her stomach that Ned could see white spots on her skin. He could never figure out what had set her off.

One day she would call him her darling boy and hug him every chance she got. But the next morning, she would stare at him silently with her small eyes that were like two blue crayon dots. Her nostrils would flare slightly, her frizzy hair would look electrified. What *had* he done, he would wonder, to make her so furious? But she never explained. Ned decided that the worst thing you could do to a person was not to say why you were angry with him.

Papa preached about only ten commandments, but

6

Mrs. Scallop had hundreds of them and she rapped them out like a woodpecker drilling away at a tree trunk.

"If you don't dry your toes well after your bath, you'll get appendicitis," she warned him. "If you drop a fork, you'll have bad news before sunset," she said. Once she had snatched the book he was reading right out of his hands, studied it closely for a second, then exclaimed, "What piffle! Talking animals, for mercy's sake! Your brains will go soft if you read such nonsense!"

Still, he preferred her woodpecker rapping to those sullen, accusing silences.

This morning had started out as a "darling boy" day. She'd described the birthday cake she was going to make for Ned on Wednesday. It would amaze him. Hadn't she made her first cake when she was a tiny thing of five? Hadn't her mother taught her good? Didn't she know how to make the best cakes for miles around? His eleventh birthday, she said, was very, very important. After you passed eleven, you had to start learning everything. If you didn't know everything by the time you were thirteen, you never got another chance.

"Well, Mrs. Scallop, I think we have more time than that," Papa had said gently.

Ned had excused himself from the table and gone upstairs to say goodbye to his mother.

"Mrs. Scallop says I have to learn everything before I'm thirteen," he had said. Mama was in her wheelchair over by the bay windows.

"I'm afraid that's what Mrs. Scallop did," Mrs. Wallis said, smiling at Ned. He saw at once that she was feeling well today. There were mornings when he had no sooner entered her room than he turned right around and left, days when she was bent over the tray table attached to the wheelchair as if a wind had pinned her there, a wind that kept her from sitting up. Those were the mornings when her fingers were as twisted as the roots of pine trees, and he would tiptoe away, feeling as if his own bones were turning into water.

"She's going to make me a birthday cake Wednesday," he'd told her.

"We'll have to grant that she bakes well," his mother said. "Although by the time she's finished a cake, by the time she tells you how absolutely wonderful it is, you hardly have any appetite left." She had turned to look out the window. "Look," she said. "It's so beautiful today. The haze hasn't formed yet. I do believe we can see all the way to West Point. I always wonder about that little island in the river. Do you suppose anyone lives on it?"

8

"You told me a story about it once," Ned had said, thinking his mother found any kind of day beautiful when she wasn't in pain.

She had laughed and exclaimed, "Oh, Ned! You remember that? You weren't much past your fifth birthday. I was still walking around. Yes . . . I made up a long story about an old man and his cat."

"Uncle Lightning," Ned said.

"Yes!"

"The cat's name was Aura."

"Aurora," she said. "That means 'goddess of the dawn.' "

She fell silent and he looked past her through the window at the river flowing between the mountains.

"Eleven is a good age to be," she said slowly. "I came to these windows just as the sun rose that morning in September, 1924, when you were born. It was a clear day, like today. Not so warm though. I wasn't thinking about the view. I loved it but I was so used to it I often looked at the mountains and the river and the sky without seeing them. That dawn, I was wondering who you were. And then, about fourteen hours later, you arrived."

He bent to kiss her goodbye and saw close up the thick braid of her fair hair that was coiled into a bun at the nape of her neck.

He had once seen Papa braiding her hair. He had

stood in the dark upper hall and looked through her
door as his Papa stood next to her wheelchair with
the hair in his hands like a great soft rope, braiding
it quickly, pinning it at her neck. Papa had then rested
his cheek on her head and Ned, suddenly shy and
uneasy, had gone on downstairs.

"We must try and be philosophical about Mrs.
Scallop," his mother had said. "She is a good cook,
and your father's mind is at ease when he must be
away."

By philosophical, Ned knew that his mother meant
they had to remind themselves there was a bright
side to Mrs. Scallop's presence in the house. It was
hard to find anything bright about Mrs. Scallop, only
red and inflamed, like skin around a splinter. Even the
rag rugs she was always braiding were without a
touch of brightness, just dull and rusty-looking.

Before she came, the Wallis family had eaten a lot
of canned salmon and canned peas. The church ladies had always tried to help out, sending hampers
of Sunday dinner home with Papa. But the ladies
tended to be partial to desserts. Large amounts of
cakes and pies and cupcakes sat around in the pantry
all week, crumbling and growing staler day by day
and nearly curing Ned's sweet tooth for good.

There had been other housekeepers over the years,

but they seemed ghostly compared to Mrs. Scallop. Ned couldn't remember what sort of meals they had made. He reminded himself, too, how relieved he was at night by the knowledge of Mrs. Scallop's presence in her bedroom off the back staircase, how comforting it was when Papa had to attend a meeting of the church deacons or visit a sick parishioner.

Even though he always lay awake until he heard the sound of the Packard's wheels on the gravel of the driveway, he wasn't frightened the way he had been so often when he was alone with his mother, imagining what would happen if the house caught on fire, or if she had a terrible attack of pain. What would he have done to help her except to get the operator on the telephone and ask her to get help? Papa had taught him to use the telephone long before he could even spell his own name.

One thing he was sure about was that if the house caught on fire while she was there, Mrs. Scallop would be able to carry both him and his mother down the stairs and out the door. She was like someone in the funny papers. He was trying to think of the name of that character when he heard the beginning of the doxology: "Praise God from whom all blessings flow . . ."

He saw Papa step back from the pulpit. He remembered now who Mrs. Scallop was like in the funnies—Powerful Katinka, who could pick up a whole trolley car!

He realized he was still holding a nickel in his hand. The deacons had forgotten to pass him the collection plate today. As the doxology died away, an elderly heartfelt voice quavered on. It belonged to Mrs. Brewster, with whom he and his father were having dinner today.

Ned stood next to Papa at the church door and shook hands with the men and bowed to the ladies. He tried to ignore Ben Smith, who was making faces at him, then ducking behind his elder brother. Ben made the most terrible faces he'd ever seen, much better than Billy Gaskell's, who was in Ned's sixth grade at school.

Ben pushed up his nose, pulled down his lower lids and stuck his tongue out, all at once. Ned felt a great single shout of laughter rising inside of himself. He turned his back on Ben and tried to concentrate on Mr. Deems hitching his mare up to the dusty old buckboard.

Later, after Papa and he had stopped to get the Sunday paper in Tyler and were driving on to Mrs. Brewster's house, Papa said, "That child, Ben Smith ... I've never seen anyone make such a face, have you? He looked exactly like a gargoyle."

Ned let out the laughter that had remained some-where inside him since Ben had made his prize face, and Papa laughed, too.

When Papa laughed like that, Ned was at once reminded of the past, the time before his mother had become ill. He imagined the three of them dancing down the living room holding hands, or skipping stones down by the Hudson River on a little muddy strip of shore where cattails grew and large damp toads hid behind rocks and the days were always sunny. He knew it couldn't have been like that; he knew it must have rained and stormed, that they hadn't spent all their time dancing and skipping stones and laughing together, yet it *felt* as though they had. It was the time he'd been happy and hadn't known it. When he was happy now, he would remind himself he was. He would say, *At this moment I'm happy*, and that was different from simply being a certain way and not having to give it a name.

Papa parked in front of the path that led to the Brewster house. It was old and narrow and leaned slightly toward a giant elm which stood next to it. A branch of the elm crossed the front of the house just beneath the two second-floor windows like a mustache.

Mrs. Brewster and her daughter welcomed them with high, wordless cries of delight. The house smelled of rat cheese and old newspapers and candle wax. Ned glanced into the small dining room and saw the food was already on the table; a great knob of butter had melted then hardened over a mountain of lumpy, mashed potatoes, and a very small joint of meat sat on a large platter. Once when they'd had Sunday dinner with the Brewsters, Ned had asked for a second helping of beef, and his father had pinched his knee and shaken his head slightly so that Ned had to say he'd changed his mind. Afterwards, Papa explained that the Brewster ladies were really as poor as church mice, and that it was best not to ask for second helpings, since you never knew what it cost people to give you a meal.

Mrs. and Miss Brewster seemed so old to Ned that it was hard for him to believe one was the daughter of the other. They both looked exactly like the women in the tintypes that were glued in an album they kept on the pine table in the living room, and which Ned always looked through when dinner was over and Papa and the Brewster ladies were speaking softly together over their coffee. Ned wasn't interested in their conversations except when his father gave a small, delicate snort of laughter. Then he knew that one of the Brewsters must have said something funny about someone in the congregation. It was the same kind of laugh Papa gave when Ned imitated Mr. Deems's extremely deep voice, or Mrs. Brewster's famous long-held note at the end of a hymn. It was not that his father was unkind—it was that he appreciated the comical side of people. In a way, Ned felt more friendly toward his father when he laughed than he did when the Reverend Wallis looked sad and described a person as being poor or miserable or brave through adversity.

Ned wandered outside the kitchen door and into the yard. Far in the distance, he glimpsed old Mr. Deems slowly traveling along the road to his farm. He was bent over the reins; the old horse bobbed along. Mr. Deems wore his long shabby dark coat, pinned at his throat with a huge safety pin. No one that Ned knew had ever seen him without that coat. He caught the hazy, grainy smell of chicken feed as a faint breeze started up, and he walked over to the small coop where the Brewsters kept a few chickens. They clucked and complained as he looked down at them. He didn't really like having Sunday dinner with people from church. It made him feel homeless, the way, he imagined, the children in the orphanage in Waterville must feel. He kicked at a stone in the grass and the hens set up an outraged cackling.

"Such a big boy," observed Miss Brewster as he

walked back into the dining room. She said it every time Ned and Papa had dinner there. "I believe it must be close to your birthday," she added. Ned was surprised; grown-ups often recalled things he thought they would have forgotten.

"Ned will be eleven on Wednesday," Papa said.

"That's a very important birthday," said Mrs. Brewster.

"All birthdays are important," observed Miss Brewster, "up to a point."

Both ladies tittered.

The sunlight fell upon the crumpled linen napkins, the flower-decorated coffee cups, the dry and thickly iced lemon cake. Mrs. Scallop, thought Ned, would have been insulted by such a cake. She was insulted several times a day—by bad weather, by stories in the newspaper, by a crow scolding from the old maple tree outside the kitchen window. "That crow is positively insulting," she had said to Ned.

He was happy to get back inside the sun-warmed Packard, to drive away from Tyler toward home. They passed through woods still dense with foliage, though the leaves were yellow and copper-colored, through open fields, a village half the size of Tyler which looked entirely deserted, then a meadow where a white dog sat on its haunches staring at five motionless cows. Soon, Ned saw the western slopes of the mountains beyond which the Hudson flowed.

Two miles after they had passed the turnoff to Waterville, the big town on the river, they reached the balm of Gilead tree under which George Washington was said to have sheltered during a thunderstorm. Papa turned off the blacktop and onto a steep dirt road. At its first sharp curve stood a tall stone house whose windows were always shuttered. Behind it was a small forest of birch trees where Ned sometimes lingered on his way home from school if he happened to be alone, not with the other children, Janet or Billy or Evelyn, who also walked home along the dirt road.

Papa told him the stone house had been empty for many years, as had the Makepeace mansion, whose land abutted the Wallis land, and like the Wallis house had been built on the crest of the hill. Eight wood columns rose from its long veranda on which stood an enormous, nearly rotted wicker settee and a rocking chair with its seat gone as though a boulder had fallen through it. Ned had looked through the dusty windows at shadowy rooms where light barely penetrated. Papa said the reason there were so many empty houses around was because of the Great Depression. The country was only beginning to recover from that terrible time because of President Franklin Delano Roosevelt. But it was too late now for many people to save their homes; often, they simply abandoned them.

It always felt a little strange to Ned to be driven along the road he was accustomed to walk—to see the small forest from the car window, and the Makepeace driveway choked with underbrush and weed, only one of its tall stone gates still upright, and to pass so quickly the rough clearing where Evelyn Kimball, a year older than Ned, lived in a big shabby house full of brothers and sisters and scrawny cats. He caught sight of Sport, the Kimball dog, running back and forth on his chain, barking at the hens that scratched in the dirt nearby. Ned knew that if a person walked straight over to Sport, he would lie down at once as though his legs were on springs and wag his tail violently. In an emergency, Mrs. Kimball would come to stay with Ned's mother, but it was hard for her to get away from home because she had so many babies, one on her hip, one hanging from her neck, and sometimes a third on her lap. At least, that's the way it seemed to Ned who was pretty sure he'd never seen her without an infant clinging to some part of her body.

They were almost home. There was the driveway,

nearly a quarter of a mile long, leading up the long slope to the house. The westering sun brought a gleam to the attic windows and struck the west side of the new lightning rods Papa had had installed recently. Right across from their driveway was old Mr. Scully's house. Ned earned thirty-five cents a week doing chores for Mr. Scully every afternoon except Sunday. Mr. Scully darned his own socks and mended his own clothes and cooked for himself. But it was getting harder for him to do heavier work, so he'd hired Ned last July to cut wood for the winter and putty up the windows and go way down the hill to the state road where Mr. Scully's mailbox was and fetch him his newspaper and the occasional post card from his daughter who lived in Seattle.

Ned loved their driveway that nearly floated away during the spring rains and filled up with rocks which bit into the worn tires of the Packard. The condition of the road was one of the two things that aroused Papa's temper; the other was the roof which always needed new shingles.

For a moment after they parked, Ned sat in a haze of sleepiness as his father lifted out his old leather briefcase from the back seat and bent over, as he usually did, to check the state of the worn tires.

"Come along, Ned . . ." his father said.

He opened his door and stepped onto the running board, then shook his head to clear away the sleepiness and raced toward a maple tree that stood on a bank below which his mother's old rock garden still flourished. He grabbed a low branch and swung out over the edge. The bells from the monastery, half a mile down toward the river, suddenly began to ring, and the week seemed to slip from Ned's back, and for no special reason, he called out, "Hurrah!" as he let go of the branch.

On the porch, next to the drooping branches of the lilac bush which was older than the house itself, stood a large yellow suitcase nearly covered with seals and stamps. Ned stared at it a second then cried, "Uncle Hilary!"

His father turned quickly away from the car. Ned pointed at the porch, and he and Papa ran up the three steps and bent over the suitcase as though it were Uncle Hilary himself. Ned put his finger on a seal that read, *Shepheard's Hotel, Cairo,* then flung himself against the screen doors which, because of the warm weather, had not yet been taken down and stored for the winter. As he walked into the central hall, he heard his mother laugh. He could tell she was happy in the special way that Uncle Hilary's visits made her happy.

20

At the end of the hall, just past the staircase, was the door to the kitchen. Mrs. Scallop stood there, her hands crossed on her stomach. "Your uncle came," she whispered to him as though it were a secret.

From now on, it was her day off. Ned knew Papa had offered to drive her into Waterville every Sunday she'd been here, but she'd never taken him up on the offer.

"I know that," said Ned. "I can hear him talking."

Mrs. Scallop withdrew slowly into the kitchen like a shadow passing into darkness. She is so *silly*, Ned thought. He started up the staircase. On the landing floor there were pools of color, reflections from the stained-glass window through which the sun poured. In the upper hall, a great pier glass leaned against the wall, and sometimes the mirror glinted as though sparks had been struck from it, or as though it had borrowed sunlight from the stained glass.

Straight ahead, its windows golden with sun, was Mama's room. She was leaning back in her wheelchair, an afghan half-fallen from her knees. Standing in front of her, thin and tall, dressed in a gray jacket nipped in at his waist, his long, narrow feet in low boots, his hair as silvery as a rain cloud, stood Uncle Hilary, one ankle crossed over the other, grinning.

They look so much alike, Ned thought; it made him feel odd to think of them as brother and sister, not only as uncle and mother. Maybe Mrs. Scallop had been right to whisper; they looked as if they had old secrets between them.

Papa had come up behind Ned. "Hilary! What a grand surprise!" he said.

"Hello, Neddy, dear," Uncle Hilary said, "And James, dear, too. I should have telephoned but I didn't know until the last minute whether I could leave New York. I had to find a place to work on my essay about the Camargue, and a friend suddenly had to go out of town and gave me his flat key and there you are! But I can only stay the night—if you don't mind putting me up, then I'll take the train down to the city in the morning. Ned! You look as though you'd grown a foot since I last saw you—let's see, has it been eleven months? Indeed, it has! And you have a birthday soon! James, you're looking well."

"I'll tell the housekeeper to make up the bed in your old room," Papa said.

Mama gave him a warning look. "It's the witching hour," she said. "Mrs. Scallop's time off. You don't want to insult her."

"I'll do it myself," Papa said.

"We all will," Uncle Hilary said, putting his arms around Ned and Papa and hugging them.

"Hilary," murmured Mama, "you change the day." Her head dropped against the back of the wheelchair; she smiled up at her brother.

She had been so nearly motionless for so many years, stuck in that chair, or wherever else Ned's father carried her, that Ned thought he'd seen everything about her. He knew her face better than anyone else's face. But he'd not seen that smile before. It seemed to tell him that she and Hilary knew a special thing that Ned couldn't know—and perhaps his Papa couldn't know, either. Ned felt jarred by anger as though someone had shoved him.

"How was dinner at the Brewsters'? Cold mashed potatoes and dry cake?" Mama asked him. He looked at the fine creases at the corners of her eyes, at the gleam of her rather large teeth. Her smile was for him now. He nodded. His anger was gone. But he felt a touch of strangeness, as though Uncle Hilary's presence had changed the day for him, too.

II

The Gun

U NCLE HILARY SAID AS THEY WENT INTO THE HALL
that it was splendid to be away from the hurly-
burly of the city, and he told Papa he was lucky to
live in an atmosphere of such meditative silence.

"What's that?" Ned asked.

"A place where you can think," Papa said, smiling
at Ned as he halted in front of a closet and collected
bed linen for Uncle Hilary.

Papa and Uncle Hilary went on to the spare bedroom, but Ned paused, noticing that the door which
led to the back staircase was open a crack. Mrs. Scallop's room was there, off the narrow landing. He
thought he glimpsed her sitting on the edge of the
iron bedstead, her stout short legs not reaching the
floor. He was pretty sure she had been listening to

them, that she often eavesdropped, and that whatever she heard filled her up like a big supper.

He stood for a while at the doorway of the spare room and listened to the pleasant rumble of his father's and uncle's voices. It was a comforting noise. The old house was so often silent. Uncle Hilary was talking about the essay he was writing about some place in the south of France. They were tucking the ends of a blanket under the mattress. Uncle Hilary suddenly leaned toward Papa and asked, "How is she really, James? She looks worn. Pain, I suppose. Isn't there anything they can do—" He looked up and saw Ned and fell silent.

"Ned knows all about his mother's condition," Papa said, looking gravely at Ned. "It's a help to me that he does," he added.

Ned was glad Papa had spoken like that to Uncle Hilary. He didn't know if his words were true, though. He knew Mama's illness got worse at times; he knew there were times, too, when she was better, when she might even be able to walk a little ways with the help of a cane. But Ned didn't really understand how their life could have so entirely changed six years ago. It almost seemed as though, overnight, they'd moved into another house in another part of the world, a house whose walls and floors were made of glass that might, if Ned wasn't very careful, shatter.

Thoughts about his mother were filling up his head, perhaps because Uncle Hilary had come. He hardly ever saw anyone with her except Papa. Mrs. Scallop didn't spend much time in her room lately except to make the bed or dust a bit or bring her the tray with her meals. Mama was very still when Mrs. Scallop was in the room, Ned had observed. People from church had used to visit quite a bit but not for the last year. He thought he knew why.

One night when he'd not been sleepy but had been lying awake in his bed, he'd heard Mama say, "Jim, please! I don't want to see them anymore. I can't bear all that *goodness*! Try to understand me . . . When someone is as helpless as I am, that goodness is like being drowned . . ." He'd puzzled over her words, wondering if what she meant was something like what he felt when Papa spoke in his preaching voice to him about someone being poor or afflicted or miserable.

He went back to Mama's door and peeked in at her. Her eyes were closed. Papa must have turned on her bedside lamp but it was weak and the room was full of shadows. Darkness was filling the windows, pressing up against them like black smoke. Through it he could see little flickers of light from

26

Waterville. Mama was sleeping. He wished she wasn't. If she'd talk to him, he might be able to stop thinking about her so hard.

Sometimes he could forget her altogether. That was especially true when he was outdoors. Then, if he happened to glance back at the house, at her windows on the second floor, he would imagine her sitting in her wheelchair, her twisted fingers and hands resting on the wooden tray that could swing out from one arm and be attached to the other so that she was imprisoned the way a baby is imprisoned in a high chair.

He could not run into her room and see her whenever he felt like it. But Papa might say, "Your mother's had her sponge bath and is feeling quite refreshed. Why don't you take up her tea to her, Ned?" He would climb the stairs wondering why the tea in the cup sloshed more and more the higher he went. He would glimpse himself in the hall mirror as he passed it, his lip caught in his teeth in anticipation of dropping the hot cup—he never had, so far—and he would walk softy into her room and place the tea in front of her, the slice of lemon in the saucer occasionally moldy because Papa hadn't had time to go to the grocer's in Waterville to get fresh lemons.

"Well, Ned," she would say, turning her gaze away

from the windows and looking at him. Some days she would smile very faintly, and he would know she was feeling bad, that that smile was all she could manage, that she had to be very careful not to move, careful the way he was with her cup of tea, so that something in her would not spill over. As far as anyone knew, she wouldn't get better; she would have good days and bad days—that was all.

There were nights when his parent's voices awoke him. Hers would be high and anguished, his father's, steady and persuasive, the way he sounded from the pulpit in church. As Ned lay listening, his room luminous with star shine or moonlight or else as dark as a well, a darkness as thick as fur pressing against his face, he knew that pain had awaked her and that his father was trying to persuade it away.

When they had fallen silent and he couldn't get back to sleep, he often walked through the house. Since Mrs. Scallop had come, he was nervous about going up the narrow splintery stairs in the back hall which led to the attic. Yet there was something thrilling about his passage there, too, a chance he might dislodge an old *National Geographic* from a heap in the dusty corner of a stair, or trip and bang his big toe, or kick over a box with a thousand old buttons in it that would cascade down the stairs right to Mrs. Scallop's threshold and scare her out of her sleep! The very thought of exploding her awake made him shudder and laugh at the same time.

In the attic, he would feel his way among the huge old trunks and boxes, the piles of books and magazines and broken furniture, to one of the small windows from which he could see the river if it was a clear night. As he stood there on tiptoe, gripping the unfinished attic windowsill in his hands, he felt as if he were the only person awake in all the great, empty night.

He would go back down the stairs and walk through the spare bedroom, past his mother's room, the small room off it where his father slept, past the hall mirror and down the stairs and into the living room with its dark wallpaper pattern of pussy willows which his grandmother, dead before he was born, had chosen, and by then his eyes were used to the dark and he could make out the glimmer of the silvery catkins. He would go into the dining room and touch the glass camel on the Tiffany shade, pass into the pantry with its smell of stale cake and sour mop and withered apples, into the big kitchen where the cracked old linoleum might nip at his bare feet like red ants. Before he went upstairs, he would pause in his father's study, testing the floorboards until he found the one that creaked. Then he would be ready to go back to his bed, to sleep.

Ned was able to visit his mother almost every day, even if it was only for a minute or two. At first, he would have a conversation with her that was not so different from the ones he had with other grown-ups, his teacher, Miss Jefferson, or members of his father's congregation like the Brewsters. If he could spend a good, long time with her, the conversation would change. He would get a little stool and take it next to the wheelchair and sit down on it. He would tell her what he had done that day, what he had seen, and even what he had thought. That was what she seemed most interested in.

When he brought her wildflowers in the spring and summer, she told him the names of each one. If he found an odd stone, she could name what minerals were in it. If he described a bird, she could sometimes tell him its name. When that was done, the flowers put aside with the stone, she would ask him what he thought.

"What's outside of everything?" he asked her once.

"The earth?"

"I mean the sky. What's outside of the sky and the stars?"

"No one knows," she said.

"There must be something," he said. "There can't be nothing, can there?"

"Your father would say God," she said.

"What would you say?" he asked, a little troubled and interested that she had a different idea than his father.

"The thought of it is too strange to fit inside my brain," she said. "Maybe it's like those dolls Uncle Hilary brought you back from Hungary when you were little. Do you remember? There must have been ten of them, each fitting inside the other until the smallest one, which was no bigger than your finger-nail. In the universe, perhaps the dolls go on forever, getting larger and larger."

He always knew when she was getting tired. He didn't know when he'd begun to learn how to tell. He would see a slight tightening of a muscle in her cheek; her shoulders would stoop. He'd get up from the stool then and kiss her cheek that was as soft as the flannel of his oldest pajamas. There was something clothlike about her skin. It made him sad for a moment though he didn't know why.

Often he didn't think about the strangeness of his mother being an invalid. But when he went to visit a school friend, or spent the afternoon with a boy from the Sunday school when his father had extra church business to take care of after services, he would be astonished at the great noise and thundering in the house, at his friend shouting, "Mom!" and banging doors and slamming windows and thumping up and down stairs. It was so different at home. He couldn't remember when he had learned to walk softly but he was pretty sure no one could make less noise than he did. If he brought someone home to play with—that did not happen often—they stayed outside or, if it was raining, on the porch.

"When did you get sick?" Ned asked Mama once when the conversation part was finished and they were really talking. He had just touched the skirt of her dress; she always wore bright, pretty dresses.

"When you were about five years old," she had answered. "But I think the sickness had been coming on for a long while."

"Before that, could you run fast?"

"Yes, I could run and run. And I rode my horse, Cosmo. I could pick you up and swing you into the air."

"Then—" he began.

"Then the ax fell," she said.

The ax fell, he repeated her words to himself now, as Mama opened her eyes and turned to look at him. She smiled. She had been like a tree, he thought, and then was cut down.

Mrs. Scallop didn't cook during her time off. One Sunday after Ned had finished his bowl of cereal and huckleberries, he had asked her what she was going to eat for supper. "Mrs. Scallop," she had replied, speaking of herself in the third person as she frequently did, "never eats supper on Sunday."

Papa made omelets that evening and sliced up some tomatoes, which he sprinkled with sugar much to Uncle Hilary's consternation. "Why is America afraid of olive oil?" he asked loudly, placing his hand on his forehead as though he had a headache. Papa smiled and didn't seem troubled by Uncle Hilary's question. Ned thought he *would* have been troubled if he'd seen Uncle Hilary winking across the table at Ned while Papa had his eyes closed and was saying grace.

After supper, Uncle Hilary and Papa sat in the living room talking and Ned lay on the floor looking at the funny papers. He always read them in the same place, between the radio and the library table. On top of the radio was a bronze sculpture of a lion, his paw raised over the head of a tiny mouse that was looking up at him, "fearlessly," Papa had said. Ned wasn't so sure about that. On the oak library table were folded newspapers which Papa kept for a week before throwing them away, a silver letter opener which had nearly turned black with tarnish, a stack of recent *National Geographic*s, a magnifying glass and a pair of library scissors inlaid with mother of pearl. Ned loved the oak table and everything that was on it. When he finished the funnies, he swung himself over to it and sat up, leaning against one of its thick legs. Papa was saying that they did lead a plain life compared to Uncle Hilary's.

"There's nothing wrong with a plain life," Uncle Hilary said with a little smile that seemed to say there *was* something wrong with it. "I get worn out by hotels and trains and languages I can't speak, and oh, my poor stomach, the things it has to put up with! Sheep's eyes and lung stew—"

"And tomatoes covered with sugar," interrupted Papa, laughing.

Uncle Hilary looked a little put out, Ned thought, as though he were the one supposed to make jokes. Then he said, "I just think it would do Ned a world of good. He's never been away from here."

"Would you like that?" Papa suddenly asked Ned, bending slightly so he could see Ned under the table's edge. "Uncle Hilary wants to take you on a trip during your Christmas vacation."

Ned's heart leaped. He wanted to shout, Yes! There was something in his father's voice that he hadn't understood; it made him uneasy. If he said yes, he wanted to go with Uncle Hilary, would Papa think he wanted to get away from him?

"Could you come, too?" he asked.

"Ned, you know I can't leave your mother," Papa said reproachfully.

"I must think of a place to take you that will fit exactly into ten days," Uncle Hilary said.

"Ned, do come out from under the table," Papa said with the special patience he had when he was trying not to be cross. Ned got to his feet.

Uncle Hilary's visits were always brief. It was probably best that way, Ned thought. He'd noticed that his father was often touchy when his brother-in-law was staying with them. Uncle Hilary did like to tease Papa—the way he had about putting sugar on tomatoes.

"The Georgia Sea Islands are too far," said Uncle Hilary pensively. "But perhaps we could manage Nag's Head."

"Well, Ned?" questioned his father.

Uncle Hilary smiled at him. He looks like electricity, thought Ned and that made him grin. "I think he'd like to go," said his uncle.

"Yes, I do want to," Ned said, looking at Papa.

"Fine, then," Papa said. He looked away from Ned,

out the window. "We'll have a harvest moon to-night," he said.

"Neddy, I must give you your birthday present. I'll be gone in the morning long before you get up for school—that is, if that old fellow, and his taxi, gets here when he should." He went out into the hall. Ned had a shelf of presents from Uncle Hilary, coins and ancient bones, a piece of oily spinach-colored jade from China, a pitcher made from lava spewed out from Mount Vesuvius, a butterfly in a glass case from Mexico and, the most valuable one of all, a bronze goat from Greece, so small Ned could hide it in his hand.

Ned went over to his father and leaned against him, and Papa took his hand and pressed it lightly. Ned didn't feel quite right. "Do you want me not to go?" he whispered.

Papa turned to look at him. "I think you'll have a fine time," he said. "I'm getting used to the idea of it now."

Uncle Hilary came back carrying a long narrow case wrapped in brown paper and tied in several placed with thick cord.

"I think he should open it," Uncle Hilary said, placing the case on the floor. Ned took the library scissors and knelt and cut the cord and pulled off the wrapping paper and lifted the top of the case.

If he had made a guess, it would have been the last thing he would have guessed, even if he'd been given one hundred chances. The room was so still he could hear the two men breathing. He picked up the air rifle and sat back on his heels.

"A Daisy," he said, looking up at his uncle, who nodded at him rapidly as though to assure him it *was* a gun he was holding.

"It's loaded," said Uncle Hilary. "All ready to go. It's time you had a boy's present instead of an old bone or a dead bug or an ancient coin that wouldn't buy you a jellybean."

"Those coins and bugs and bones and carvings you brought Ned were splendid," Papa said loudly, "tokens, clues to the past, signs for guessing and imagining."

"Happy Birthday, Ned," Uncle Hilary said uncertainly.

"What is there to imagine with a gun?" asked Papa in the same loud voice. "Hilary, your gift is not quite the thing . . ."

Ned's hands tightened on the gun.

"Something dead," Papa said more quietly. "That's what there is to imagine with a gun."

"I had thought of target practice," Uncle Hilary said stiffly. "I had thought of skill and a trained eye—"

"Perhaps in a few years," his father said as though his uncle hadn't spoken. "When you reach your fourteenth birthday, Ned, if you still want to learn to shoot—"

"Papa," protested Ned, "don't you remember when you took me to the fair? You let me try at the rifle range and the man said I had a true eye and a steady hand. Don't you remember that?"

"That was a game," Papa said. "Oh, Hilary! Really, you should have asked me about this!"

"I had thought, James, you would be overjoyed if Ned brought down one of those chipmunks that has been dining on your roof timbers. You complain endlessly about them . . ."

"That's just what I don't want him to do," Papa said. His voice took on a conciliating tone. "Hilary, I know Ned appreciates your generosity. I do, too. But I must say no this time. I'll put the gun away. Ned can have it when he's older."

Papa reached for the Daisy. As Ned handed it to him, he thought for a moment the two men might start to fight. Uncle Hilary had taken a step toward Papa as though to snatch the gun away from him. Papa's jaw was thrust out, his eyes narrowed. Then Uncle Hilary said, "I'm sorry to have made this difficulty." He left the living room at once. Ned listened to his rapid footsteps going upstairs.

"I know you're disappointed, Ned," Papa said softly. He placed his hand on Ned's shoulder. It felt like a stone.

"I ask you to trust me, Ned," he said.

Ned was staring at the engraving on the gun which Papa was holding, barrel down, in his other hand. It looked like a large bird in flight.

"Will you trust me?" his father asked again, more insistently.

The room seemed to have grown almost unbearably hot. Ned nodded slowly. His father withdrew his hand, and Ned went over to the radio and drew a finger down the muscular back of the bronze lion. The finger came up covered with dust. He imagined Mrs. Scallop saying, "Mrs. Scallop doesn't dust lions."

"There are so many accidents with guns, Ned. People are blinded, maimed."

"I would only have shot at old tin cans," Ned said. "I wouldn't shoot a chipmunk."

He turned from the lion and saw on his father's face an expression he didn't like. It was the sympathy that was often there when he said no to something Ned wanted. The *no* was bad enough; the sympathy was awful.

"Take your mind away from it. There'll be other presents," Papa said.

Ned nodded, knowing that if he didn't, his father would keep him in the room until he did. His father insisted on agreement, whatever else had happened. Ned went upstairs to go to the little room over the porch that Papa had said he could use for a study. As he walked through the hall, he saw that his mother's room was dark but there was a line of light beneath Uncle Hilary's door. In his study, he flung himself on the old horsehair sofa Papa had dragged in there. He looked at the table where there were piles of post cards, some of them from Uncle Hilary, others which he'd found in the attic. His stamp album was on the floor open to the page for stamps from Ruanda-Urundi. It was blank. He stared at the shelf where Uncle Hilary's presents from over the years were lined up. There was nothing to do with them; they just sat there, looking dusty.

He heard his father's footsteps going up to the attic. Then that's where he was taking the gun. His father wouldn't hide it. The painful thing was that, though Ned didn't always trust his father, his father trusted him, and that seemed to him unfair, although he couldn't explain why it was so.

The one thing in the world that would make him feel better right now was to have that gun in his hands once more, to feel the weight of it, to examine every inch of it closely. If he could do that only once, he would turn his mind from it as his father had told him to do.

There was no door to Ned's study, just a heavy old velvet curtain on rungs. Papa pushed it aside and stuck his head in.

"Good night, dear Ned," he said.

"Good night, Papa."

"Don't stay up too late."

Gradually the night sounds of the old house faded away until all that was left was the creaking and sighing of the boards and joists, the old timbers. By the light of the orange moon that seemed twice as big as usual, he could see clearly the boughs of the maple tree. In a wind, even a slight breeze, they would click up against the window of his study. Papa was always saying he ought to prune the tree, but Ned loved the sound the branches made.

He had always been so glad when Uncle Hilary visited. But not this time. He rolled off the horsehair sofa and onto a long patch of light on the floor. A coin fell out of his trouser pocket. It was the nickel that hadn't been collected from him in church that morning. The morning felt a week away. He shot the nickel into a corner of the room the way he would have shot an aggie. He didn't bother to look for it.

41

The harvest moon had filled the whole house with pools and streams and narrow ribbons of light. As Ned wandered from window to window, holding his shoes in his hand so he wouldn't make any noise, he lost track of time; the house seemed to float above the long meadows that ran down toward the Hudson and the north field edged by the grove of pines in whose branches Ned had often sat in the summer, reading a book. From the living room bay windows, he thought he could just make out the chalk-white ghostly Makepeace mansion beyond the far line of maples to the south.

Leaning against the oak library table, he could see the dark narrow buildings of the asylum across the Hudson. Papa had taken him there once when he'd had to visit a parishioner who'd set fires all over the village of Tyler.

Ned remembered playing with a wooden horse beneath a great elm tree while his father was in the red brick ward with its porches screened heavily with black wire, and how he'd looked up once and thought he'd seen a round pale face gazing down at him like a small moon.

Though it was still warm from the day's heat, Ned shivered as though feeling winter's chill. He went through the central hall to the kitchen. At the back stairs, he stood for a long time listening.

His scalp tingled. He began to climb, holding his breath as he went past Mrs. Scallop's room. Out of the corner of his eye, he saw her lying in her bed, a small mound like a risen cake in the oven, and he heard a faint fluttering of the air that was nearly a snore.

He went up the attic stairs on all fours, moving cautiously through the heaps of magazines. The orange had drained out of the moon; the light was pale now, weaker, but enough to show the hills of books and boxes and trunks and cases and crates and baskets.

The gun was not among them but in an unfinished room in the corner of the attic. Ned found it almost at once, as though it had a voice which had called to him.

He could hear his heart thudding as he squatted and rested his hands on the case. After a while, he made his way to the head of the attic stairs and listened.

He went back to the little room, opened the case and took out the Daisy rifle. He gripped it in his hands and stood up and went to the stairs and made his way all the way down to the kitchen without making one sound. He balanced the gun against the wall and went back upstairs to get his shoes.

When he was outdoors and well away from the porch, he sat down on the ground and put on his shoes. He knew now that he would have to try the gun just once. Then he would be able to do what his father had told him to do—take his mind away from it.

He glanced back at the house. Its shadow, enormous, black, nearly shapeless, lay on the ground. All around him were the smaller shadows of trees.

He began to follow the driveway as it curved out of sight of the house toward the small stable where Papa kept the Packard in bad weather. The tracks were almost completely overgrown with weeds and brush by the time the driveway reached the stable. It was really an old barn, much older than the house. Rough-hewn stones formed its foundation; ivy had straggled over much of its half-collapsed roof. Mama had told him that Cosmo, her black gelding, had been stabled there, and that at night she used to listen for his soft neigh and the thump of a hoof hitting the stable floor.

The night sky had changed; thin clouds drifted across the face of the moon. A slight breeze sprang up for a brief moment and rustled the tall grass that grew at the base of the stable. Grass grew inside, too. It wouldn't be so long, Papa had said, before the stable would simply fall into the ground and become part of it—another thing he should take care of that he simply hadn't the time or money to do.

Ned's hearing had sharpened. He could hear the sleepy night sounds of birds, the rustle of field mice or voles, or perhaps a raccoon, as they moved about in the dry grass of the fields.

He lifted the gun to his shoulder just as he remembered lifting it at the shooting range Papa had taken him to when they went to the fair. He sighted along its barrel, pointing it first at the pines, then turning very slowly in a wide circle which followed the eastern range of the mountains, the river, the western bulge of Storm King Mountain; he aimed it high above the maple trees which partly hid the Makepeace mansion, brought it to the slope behind which stood his own house, all the way back until he had turned completely around and was facing the side of the stable.

As he blinked and opened his right eye wide, he saw a dark shadow against the stones which the moon's light had turned the color of ashes. For a split second, it looked alive. Before he could think, his finger had pressed the trigger.

There was a quick *whoosh*, the sound a bobwhite makes when it bursts out of underbrush, then silence. He was sure there hadn't been any loud report that would have waked anyone in the house, yet he had heard something, a kind of thin disturbance in the air. He walked over to the barn. There was no shadow now. There was nothing. He might have only dreamed that he had fired the rifle.

He felt tired, dull, as he trudged along the drive toward the house. It seemed a long time before he would be able to crawl under his sheet and go to sleep. He felt the gun hanging loosely at his side. He'd lost all interest in it.

As he came in sight of the house, nearly lost in the darkness now, for clouds filled the sky, he glanced up at the attic where he would have to carry the gun and replace it in its case.

He stood absolutely motionless. He was sure there was a face there, pressed against the glass, looking down at him the way the person had looked down at him through the heavy black wire screen of the asylum years before.

III

The Old Man

"HAPPY BIRTHDAY, NED," HIS MOTHER SAID. SHE WAS dressed and in her wheelchair. He could see from the door that she was holding something in her hands. "Come here to me," she said.

Some mornings he walked to school and some mornings Papa drove him in the Packard. What was unvarying was that his mother's door was closed when he tiptoed past it, his school books under his arm, and went downstairs to his breakfast. He could not remember her ever having been up this early to wish him *Happy Birthday*. It meant that Papa had risen very early to do her hair and help her dress and carry her to the chair. He dropped his books on the bed as he went to her. He felt shy; he wasn't accustomed to seeing her at the start of his day.

Her hands opened. On her palms lay a gold pocket watch nearly as flat as a wafer, its chain wound round her fingers like a golden grass snake.

"This watch was my father's," she said. "Now it's yours." She lifted it up to him. He took it and held it to his ear. It ticked softly. "You can keep it by your bedside for now. When you go away to college, you can carry it in your pocket. You'll always know what time it is."

He looked at her hands as he did every day. Her thumb joints were more swollen than they had been yesterday. "Thank you, Mama," he said.

"I think you were too little when you saw your grandfather to remember him. I know how glad he would have been to know that you have his watch. His initials are on the back, do you see? He was given it when he retired from the newspaper in Norfolk."

The watch felt warm in his hand as though it were alive.

"Uncle Hilary left an *écu* for you. Papa has it. It's a gold coin from France, very old. I think this is a golden birthday." She smiled. He thought she looked uncertain. He sensed she wanted to say something more and was searching for words. He felt a sudden impatience and wished he was gone, out of the house and on his way. It was something he didn't often

48

feel when he was with her. But he had waked up that way, uneasy and in a hurry.

"He was sorry about the gun," she said slowly, looking down at her hands. "He realized he should have spoken to your father first—before giving it to you."

Ned felt his face turn red. She was looking at him now. He didn't meet her eyes. "I don't like guns either," she said softly. "I'm afraid of them." Standing there silently, unable to speak, he felt he was lying to her. "Oh, Ned!" she exclaimed, "I'm sorry, too!"

"I have to go," he mumbled, and backed away out of the room and ran downstairs.

His class sang "Happy Birthday" to him. Some of the boys snickered and some of the girls giggled. Miss Jefferson had brought cookies she had made and a basket of Jonathan apples. In honor of Ned, she read a chapter from *The Call of the Wild* by Jack London. It was stuffy in the classroom, as hot as though it were still August. The other children looked at him, then at each other, and grinned from time to time, the way they always did when it was someone's birthday, as if it were a thing a person had done, accomplished. It isn't anything at all, he said to himself, just a day that comes along.

In the evening, Mrs. Scallop brought the cake she had made for him up to Mama's room. Papa carried a big pitcher of fresh lemonade and Ned's presents. Miss Brewster had sent him *Treasure Island*, and the Ladies' Aid Society of the church had sent an anthology of poems by Rudyard Kipling. Papa gave him a new winter coat, a book called *Robin Hood and His Merry Men* and an atlas so he could learn where the countries were which his stamps came from.

"You must blow out all the candles or a strange fate will befall you," warned Mrs. Scallop.

His mother laughed loudly. "Oh, Mrs. Scallop!" she exclaimed. "A strange fate befalls us all!"

Ned blew them out. Everyone clapped and he cut pieces of the cake and handed them around. Mrs. Scallop presented him with the most hideous rug, Ned thought, of all the rugs he'd seen her make. It would look nice beside his bed, she said, cozy to walk on when the weather changed. Ned was glad when he could be alone in his room. He found a pile of animal stories he had cut out of the newspapers over the years and kept in an old shoe box. He felt slightly embarrassed at his age to be still reading Thornton Burgess, but it was comforting to gaze for a long time at an illustration of the plump rabbit standing in front of a tree or in a vegetable patch. His birthday was nearly over. The house grew silent except for the leaking of the toilet flush which his father was never able to repair permanently.

Suddenly he tore up the handful of stories and dropped the pieces into his wastebasket. The gold watch ticked on his dresser, his new books piled up beside it. It had really been a very hard day. He knew it was all because of the gun, his worry over what he had done. In just a few days, that worry had come to be part of whatever he was thinking about. Had he really seen a face that night looking down at him from a window in the house? If he had, it must have been Mrs. Scallop's face. But if it had been she—and if she had noticed the gun—why hadn't she said anything? Perhaps he had been carrying the gun in such a way she couldn't have seen it. Had the rifle made a much louder noise than he had thought and waked her up?

As though it had slid into the room, the wall of the stable appeared before him; he saw a flicker of movement, or moonlight wavering, or breeze-bent wild grass, something that drew the gun to it and made his finger press the trigger. He shook his head and it disappeared. He wished Uncle Hilary hadn't come.

Papa had said—take your mind away from it. It had gotten *into* his mind. He could tell Papa what he had done. After all, Papa wouldn't strap him the way he'd heard Billy Gaskell's father strapped him for the slightest thing. No, Papa would only look grave, disappointed. But he'd forgive him.

Ned put his head under the pillow. At some point, he fell asleep.

For four more Sundays the heat held. The flowers arranged around the pulpit wilted in an hour. Old Mr. Deems, dazed by the heat, snored so loudly the sound of it cut like a buzz saw through the hymns. And on the way home from church, the wind that blew through the windows of the Packard felt as though it had come straight from an oven.

When Ned ate his early Sunday supper on the porch, the sky flared like fire, and the monastery bells, ringing for vespers, seemed to be working their way through hot tar.

He went up to visit his mother. A palmetto fan lay on her tray and she was drooped over it. He fanned her for a few minutes. She smiled her gratitude. "A person can imagine anything except weather," she murmured.

The river was ink-blue and looked as unmoving as water in a basin.

"Are you all right, Neddy?" Her question took him by surprise. She had spoken urgently, and although her words were ordinary, they pierced him as if they'd flown straight to the painful place in his mind.

"I have to write a poem about autumn," he said hurriedly. "It's supposed to be for tomorrow and I haven't done it yet."

She rested her head against the back of the wheel chair and looked at him silently.

"Well, what I thought was that I'd write about the gypsies Papa and I saw today, just where the Waterville road is, two caravans"—he paused for a moment, staring at the interest that had come into her eyes as plain to see as a light going on—"and lots of thin black dogs running around, and children, and the women all dressed in bright clothes. Papa says they usually come in October."

"That's a wonderful idea, Ned," she said. "Gypsies in the fall."

He *did* have a homework assignment but he didn't have to hand it in for a week, and it wasn't a poem but a nature description. He'd been able to trick his mother. It made him feel a little sick.

A lie was so tidy, like a small box you could make

with nails and thin pieces of wood and glue. But the truth lay sprawled all over the place like the mess up in the attic. At the thought of the attic, of the unfinished room and what lay in it, he felt as though a giant hand had been clapped over his mouth.

His mother was staring at him. He suddenly knew she was trying to *read* his face, and he felt a strange burst of relief. He hadn't quite convinced her; in a way he couldn't understand, that made him feel safer.

The next morning, the last Monday in October, started off hot, but Ned felt something different in the air. Perhaps it was the absolute stillness of the leaves and the blades of grass—a kind of waiting.

Ned, and the children he walked home with most afternoons, crossed the hot asphalt of the state road quickly, then drifted apart as they went up the steep curving dirt road. Ned glanced longingly at the stone house, so cool and mysterious-looking. Billy Gaskell, who was Ned's age but taller and heavier than he, began to pick up pebbles and fling them ahead. They sent up puffs of smoke where they landed, and Evelyn Kimball, whose shoelaces were often untied and whose hair never looked combed, shrieked as though she were being pinched each time Billy flung a pebble. But Janet Hoffman, thin as the long pigtail that hung down her back, trudged along the road off by herself. Ned wished Evelyn would shut her mouth. She made the heat worse. He wandered over to the ditch thinking he would pause there and let everyone get ahead. There was an interesting-looking stick lying on the ground. As he bent to pick it up, it wriggled quickly away. He glanced further along the ditch. He saw two more snakes. One was orange and brown like the first, the other was white with green wedge-shaped markings.

"Ooh! Snakes!" breathed Evelyn, coming to stand next to him.

Billy lumbered toward them. "What're you looking at?" He saw the snakes. Like lightning, he bent over and grabbed one. "Take out the fangs!" he cried.

Everything happened fast. Janet put her head down and aimed herself at Billy's belly like a small goat and knocked him flat on the ground. The snake flew out of his hand, landing in the high grass on the other side of the ditch, and curled itself away out of sight. "Snakes are human, too!" Janet yelled. "You big bully!" She sat down on Billy, her skinny, scabby knees clutching him around his thick waist, and grabbed his lank brown hair, pulled up his head and let it bang back on the road.

Billy heaved himself up. Janet tumbled onto the

road and Evelyn grabbed her arms and pulled her to her feet, spanking the dust from her dress. Ned was astonished to see that Billy was grinning. Then he started laughing, bending over himself and smacking his knees.

"Yah!" jeered Evelyn. "You got it this time, Billy. And from a nine-year-old girl. Ha! Ha!"

Billy was unperturbed. He marched on down the road, his big shoulders somewhat stooped, looking, Ned thought, like the buffalo engraved on the nickel. He lived a good mile beyond Ned's turnoff, and nobody ever drove him to school, no matter what the weather was like. Janet's path through the woods was already in sight. Just before she turned off to it, Ned said admiringly, "That was pretty good—what you did. But snakes aren't really human."

"They're alive," she said.

"Billy's too dumb to know he got beat up," Evelyn said as she kept step with him. Billy was far ahead of them now. "My daddy says the heat drives the snakes down from the mountains," she went on. "I saw two in the yard near the henhouse."

"Why'd he want to take their fangs out?"

"Those old snakes don't even have fangs. They ain't poisonous. He's mean. He just wanted to do something to them."

"But—why?" Ned muttered.

"Did you see the way Janet got him down! He didn't even try to fight her back. And he's twice as big. Big old dumb boy . . ."

She stumbled over a hummock of earth and the dust flew up around her. He looked at her face with its slanty pumpkin eyes as she righted herself. As long as he could remember, the Kimballs had been living in their big, ramshackle house, and he and Evelyn had walked home from school together since he'd been eight. But she'd never spoken to him so much before. The snakes had made her talkative. He knew his mother liked Mrs. Kimball. When she came to take care of Mama, he'd heard Mrs. Kimball call her "precious," and "dear heart." Mr. Kimball was a carpenter but he didn't get much work. Papa had once said he couldn't think how the poor man provided for all those children.

"I chase the chickens sometimes," Evelyn said to him in a confiding voice. "They run and squawk like they're crazy."

"But you don't hurt them, do you?"

"No. I just scare them. Ma wrings their neck and we eat them."

"That must hurt."

"Well . . . it finishes them." She burst into a shout

of laughter. "That Janet! Skinny little beetle like that!" She waved and turned off up the road to the Kimball yard where chickens scratched in the earth around old car parts and piles of planks. Ned saw a raggedy little boy wearing a man's shirt sitting on an up-turned washtub. "Evie!" he shouted. "Evie is home!"

Ned turned left off the dirt road to the path he'd worn through the field that went all the way down to the state road, several hundred yards below, where Mr. Scully's mailbox stood, nailed to a splintery post. He took the Waterville newspaper and the one letter out of the mailbox and went back up the hill to Mr. Scully's house. He knocked on the kitchen door. Pretty soon he heard Mr. Scully moving inside like a mouse in a paper sack. Through the screen, whose rusty grid kept out horseflies but not houseflies, Ned could smell wood ash and dried apples.

"Hello, Ned," Mr. Scully said. He was standing just behind the screen, a small stooped man dressed as always in an old green and black plaid wool shirt and black trousers. He opened the door suddenly, and Ned had to jump off the step then jump back on it and scoot inside before the screen door swung to. Mr. Scully stared at the letter in Ned's hand. Al-though most of the time he moved as slowly as molasses moves across a plate, he snatched up his spectacles from the kitchen table and held out his hand for the letter. He peered at it and sighed. "Bother! It's only a doctor bill," he said. Ned knew he was always hoping to hear from his daughter, Doris, who had gone out West years ago.

It was dark in the kitchen. There was one window and it was dirty. Mr. Scully wouldn't turn on any kind of light, electric or kerosene, until nightfall. Ned began his chores. He pumped water to wash the dishes Mr. Scully had left in the chipped enamel basin from his supper last night and his breakfast and lunch to-day. There were a cup, two plates, a small pot, a frying pan, two forks and a sharp little knife with a blade worn thin. When he finished washing up, Ned swept out the kitchen and the parlor. Though Mr. Scully had plenty of wood chopped and stored in the shed, he might ask Ned to break up kindling. He worried about having enough wood for the cold weather. Some afternoons Ned made up his bed. Mr. Scully didn't use sheets, only blankets. After that, it would be time to go through Mr. Scully's boxes. They usually managed two a week. The boxes were piled up in the parlor where Ned had stacked them after bringing them down from the attic.

"Once I was young David Scully. Now I'm old

David," he'd told Ned when he first decided to sort through all his things. "It's time I put my house in order," he had said. Whenever a post card turned up in a box, he'd give it to Ned for his collection. Most things he put into old pillowcases to be thrown away.

Mr. Scully could still drive his old Model A down the dirt road to the state road and two miles further to a small general store to pick up groceries. He could still make his own bread, and his applesauce. But he was worried, Ned knew, about how much longer he'd be able to take care of himself. He was afraid of winter.

The house was very old and hadn't been much to start with; the floors creaked, and the window frames were nearly rotted away. When the wind blew, it sifted through the house as though it had been a sieve. When Mr. Scully's daughter had come East last time, she'd had inside plumbing put in the house, and she'd bought a gas stove and a refrigerator for him. Mr. Scully wouldn't give up the kitchen pump though. And he never put a thing in the refrigerator. He had said to Ned once, a bit grudgingly, that the water closet was an improvement over the out-house.

Still, the old man could do a great deal for himself.

Ned had come to realize, after working for him several months, that Mr. Scully really wanted company an hour or so a day. He had enough wood for ten winters.

"One of these days, we'll have to clean up that yard," Mr. Scully said. He and Ned peered through the dusty window. The yard did look pretty bad. There was a heap of tires, all worn smooth, a rusty scythe leaning up against a tree, the discarded icebox just beneath the shed roof, an old ragged quilt piled on top of it, and many other objects that were gradually becoming indistinguishable from the ground itself.

"How old are you, Ned? I know you must have told me. I forget so much."

"I'm just eleven," Ned replied. "My birthday was last month."

"I'm sixty-nine years older than you," said Mr. Scully. He pursed up his mouth as though to whistle but gave a tight little laugh instead.

The leaves on the maple tree just outside the window were brown and spotted like the skin on Mr. Scully's hands and forehead.

"You notice how the days are getting shorter? Soon, it'll be Thanksgiving. Look at those crows out there. They know winter's coming."

Ned put the dishes he'd washed on the tin counter to drain. There was no drying cloth. It was hard to imagine winter now, hard to imagine all the fields as bare as the breadboard that hung from a nail behind the pump.

The old man was fussing with the gas flame of his new stove that sat next to the big black Franklin stove he used in the winter to heat the kitchen. He was making tea as he always did for himself and Ned. He would add a few drops to his cup from a small bottle he kept on his shelf with his canned goods. "Rum," he'd told Ned on the first day Ned had come to work for him. "To make me warm. When you're old, it's hard to keep warm."

When the chores were done, they would begin to sort through a box in the parlor. When he'd put aside trash to be burned or old clothes to give away, Mr. Scully would pick up the mementos he had saved and tell Ned about them. Ned understood that that was what Mr. Scully wanted most—for Ned to listen to his history.

"See this stone?" he said, after he'd filled a sack with old newspaper clippings about the sinking of the Titanic, remarking that he couldn't think why he'd saved them in the first place. "It's a soapstone actually. Look how it's carved." He put it in Ned's hand.

The soapstone had an oily feel to it. Ned couldn't make out what the carving was.

"It's Chinese, and the symbols mean good luck. Well—I'm giving you that for your birthday—even though it's past. My poor uncle wouldn't have agreed there was much luck in the stone. He was in the San Francisco earthquake. When they pulled him up from under his house, the stone was embedded in his chest. It's a pagan thing. I can't think why he was wearing it." He laughed suddenly. It was more of a cackle than a laugh, Ned thought.

"Thank you," he said. It made him feel queer, knowing the stone had been buried in a man's chest almost thirty years ago.

"Imagine!" exclaimed the old man. "Everything you touch in this world has a history. Drink your tea. It'll cool you off. Did you know that hot tea cools a person? Life is full of paradox."

They looked through the black pages of an album thickened with tintypes and yellowed photographs. Mr. Scully turned the pages very slowly. "My mother," he said, pointing to a tinted tintype of a young girl with a thick frizz of hair on her forehead. "I hadn't even been born when that was taken," he said meditatively. "Life is strange." He pointed to another of a man in a uniform, leaning on a gun. "There's my father."

"Why does he have a gun?" asked Ned.

"It was during the Civil War. My father fought in it and was killed by it. He was wounded in the Antietam campaign in the battle on South Mountain on September 14, 1862, and he came home to die. I was six years old, Ned. I can see him now, as clear as I can see you, lying in the bed in our house in Poughkeepsie. His face was as white as the bed linen. My mother was bending over him when I came into their room. Her hand was stretched out over his forehead. I remember how thin her fingers were, how her wedding ring slipped forward to the knuckle, how white my father's skin was next to that living healthy hand. Then she pressed it to his face."

He looked up suddenly and sniffed the air. "The weather's changing. I can feel a storm coming up."

Ned would have liked to know more about the battle on South Mountain. He stared down at the gun in the tintype. A remembrance of the feeling of a gun came to him.

"He looks so proud, don't he? Maybe it was because he was holding his head so stiff and serious. Just think! Some Southern boy that was going to kill him may have been getting his picture took, too, in his uniform and leaning on *his* gun." He closed the album. "I'll keep this," he said.

Mr. Scully looked tired; his jaw had fallen open slightly. At times, his speech would grow slurred as though a sponge were being passed over his words. Ned took their cups out to the kitchen and washed them. The sky had darkened but there was still a glow of sunlight on the distant hills that rose up on the other side of the state road.

He put the cups on the counter. Next week, maybe, he'd start cleaning up the yard. As he looked through the window, thinking of where he would begin, he saw a gaunt cat move slowly away from the out-house.

"There's a cat in the yard," he called out to Mr. Scully.

"I get one once in a while," said the old man from the parlor. "Some of them live in the woods up your way. Feral cats—gone wild. They do all right in the warm months but winter kills most of them off."

Ned watched the cat a moment.

"There's something wrong with this one. It looks sick," he said.

He heard Mr. Scully groan as he got to his feet, then shuffle into the kitchen. Ned had noticed that he was wearing his slippers. He must not be feeling too well today, Ned knew. If he had been, he would have worn his black shoes that buttoned up the side. He came up next to Ned and leaned toward the window.

"He looks like he's already been through the winter," Mr. Scully said. "Poor devil. Take some of that loaf and break it up into pieces and pour a little milk on them," he directed Ned. "You can use that bowl and set it outside near the shed. He does look wild."

The cat was as gray as a mole and its fur was matted. As it peered toward the house, it shook its head constantly as though to clear away something that made seeing difficult.

"What's the matter with him?" Ned asked.

"Hunger," replied Mr. Scully. "No. Wait a minute. There is something wrong."

"One of its eyes is shut tight."

The cat came closer to the house.

"The eye isn't there," Ned said. "There's just a little hole." He felt a touch of fear.

Mr. Scully pressed against the counter. Ned could feel his breath.

"You're right," Mr. Scully said. "The cold does that to them sometimes, and he looks big enough to have been born last year. Or else someone used him for target practice. A boy would do that. A living target is more interesting than a tin can. Or he might have been in a bad fight with another animal."

"That looks like dried blood on his face," Ned

said. His voice sounded odd to him, far away. He took the bowl with the bread and milk and went out to the shed and placed the bowl just inside it, near the stacked wood. As he stood up, a faint breeze stirred the hot air, then it died away.

The stillness was deep as though the earth itself had drawn in its breath. The only thing moving was a wasp near the roof of the outhouse. Ned watched it as its circles grew smaller and smaller until, all at once, it disappeared. Probably its nest was there just under the roof. Maybe there were snakes in back of the outhouse where the tangled grass grew thick. He suddenly recalled how Janet had flung her whole self against Billy, how the snake had flown out of his hands. A thought was buzzing and circling inside his head, a thought that stung like a wasp could sting.

Mr. Scully had said wild cats lived up in the woods among the thick-boughed trees where Ned had read books in the summer. Between the house and the woods was the old stable.

Ned had taken the gun and fired it. He had seen something move along the stones of the foundation. It hadn't been tall grass stirring in a current of air. It had been something living. He had disobeyed his father and he had shot at something that was alive. He knew it was that cat. What would Janet have done to him if she had seen him that night, shooting at something he had told himself was a shadow. Had he really thought it was a shadow? Would a shadow make you feel so alert? Sharpen your hearing? Make your heart drum?

Years ago, the church ladies had outdone themselves and packed a hamper of cakes for his father's birthday. Papa had brought the hamper home and put the cakes on the kitchen table, five of them. Papa had said, "The left hand didn't know what the right hand was doing. I can't *think* why they don't plan things a little better!" and shaken his head. He'd taken three of the cakes to the Kimballs and one to Mr. Scully but he kept the chocolate cake. Ned, who loved chocolate better than anything, had gotten up after everyone was asleep and gone down to the kitchen and eaten handfuls of cake until he could hardly stand up. He was sick the next morning and stayed home from school.

He recalled exactly how it had been, standing in the dark, the cake moist in his hands, stuffing pieces of it into his mouth, knowing he shouldn't be doing what he was doing, but shutting his eyes tight with the joy of it.

In the morning, as he clutched his belly, Papa had pulled a chair to the side of his bed and sat down and spoken to him in an especially gentle voice, that spooky voice he used when he was trying to teach Ned something. "I know it was good," Papa had said. "Just because a thing is good doesn't mean we can have as much of it as we want."

He hadn't been able to figure out at first how his father had known what he'd done. Later, when he was able to creep downstairs, he saw the crumbling ruins of the cake on its plate.

"Come here, my little hog," his mother had said. "I understand you made a chocolate cake miraculously disappear during the night."

Thinking about that now, remembering how he'd put his face down on his mother's lap, how he'd said he'd *never* do that again, and how she'd touched his hair and said, "Yes, that's what we always say," he realized how childish it all had been. How childish all the bad things he'd ever done were compared to what he'd done on the night of Uncle Hilary's visit.

He looked around the yard. The cat was gone. He hoped he'd never see it again. He went back into the kitchen.

"The storm is closer," Mr. Scully said. Standing next to him, Ned stared at his soft old mouth, his stained teeth, and smelled his dried-leaf-and-old-wood smell.

"I left the bowl for the cat," he said.

"Hunting will be hard for him now. These cats live pretty good off rodents until the ground freezes over. I'll keep food out for him. Maybe he'll manage."

Ned didn't think he would. He'd seen the gap, the dried blood, the little worm of mucus in the corner next to the cat's nose where the eye had been.

He walked slowly up the long road home. The house in the pale storm-light looked like a picture of a castle in a book. He couldn't remember from which window that face had looked out at him that night. It might not have been a face, after all, he thought; it might have been the old gondolier's hat which hung from a nail in the attic. The hat couldn't have moved itself to a window. It must have been Mrs. Scallop. It seemed to him now that if she'd seen him carrying the gun, she would, somehow, know about the cat. Yet it wasn't like her—not to let him *know* what she knew. He shivered suddenly the way he did when Papa opened the cellar door.

He stayed on the porch a moment looking down at the river. A single line of birds drew a black thread across the swelling gray clouds. His mother would know what kinds of birds they were. She was prob-

70

ably watching them, too, from the bay windows. Suddenly, he wanted to see her more than anything in the world.

"Come in, Neddy," whispered Mrs. Scallop from behind the screen door. "I have some nice cold milk for you. How's Mr. Scully? He looked very feeble to me when I saw him last week puttering around his house. They'll come to take him away one of these days."

He didn't want to ask her but he did. "Who? Take him where?"

"Ah, well . . ." she said, sighing. He pushed open the screen door and she backed slowly away toward the kitchen entrance. He clenched his jaw; he wouldn't ask her again. As he put his hand on the newel post of the staircase, she said softly, "To the old folks home, of course. That's what happens to all of us when we get old and useless. Yes, Ned. That's why I'm so tolerant of folks. What I say is—people suffer enough in this life. Why should I add to their suffering? But then I'm like that—I wear my heart on my sleeve."

Ned took the stairs two at a time.

"Don't be so noisy!" thundered Mrs. Scallop. "Think of your poor mother!"

Mama was looking toward the river. A tremendous longing rose up in him. If she would only stand and walk to him and put her arms around him! He had seen her walk—not only in memory or in dreams—but with the help of a cane and Papa's arm. But so rarely!

She turned to look at him. She barely lifted the fingers of her left hand from the tray to wave at him. He walked to her. "Ned," she said, saying his name strongly the way she would say *yes* or *river*.

"Mrs. Scallop says that Mr. Scully is going to be taken away to the old folks home," he told her. "She said she wears her heart on her sleeve."

"Mrs. Scallop knows nothing about the future," she said, touching Ned's wrist with her warm, crooked fingers, "and you must beware of people who wear their hearts on their sleeves; it's not the natural place to keep your heart—it turns rusty and thin, and it leaves you hollow inside."

There was a book on the tray, *Middlemarch*. "What's that about?" he asked, suddenly very tired. He felt his shoulders droop. Even his knees felt tired.

"Nearly everything," she said. "It is about lives. I think you've had a hard day, Ned. Is there something on your mind? Something worrying?"

There was a good deal on his mind. His mother's fingers had slipped from his wrist. What if he told her about the cat? He imagined how she would look if he told her—horrified!

Mr. Scully had said the winter cold could affect their eyes. It might have been in a fight, just as the old man had suggested. If the cat came back to the yard while he was there, maybe he would get a closer look. Maybe the eye was there after all! Maybe another cat had scratched its lid so severely it only looked as if the eye had been torn out.

"There's Papa," said his mother. Ned heard the Packard struggling up the long slope and rounding the north side of the house where his father would park it beneath the crab apple tree. But the car didn't stop. Ned realized Papa was driving it to the stable.

"I'm glad he's home," said his mother. "I think we're going to have a fierce storm."

Mrs. Scallop was muttering in the doorway.

"Speak up, Mrs. Scallop!" Mama said sharply. "I'm not dead yet!"

"Oh—I was just saying, Ned's milk will be all warm the way he don't like it."

Mama gave him a conspiratorial smile and said in a low voice, "Better go down and drink it . . ."

He felt almost happy, suddenly, and he went swiftly past Mrs. Scallop, down the stairs to the hall where he met his father carrying two large bags of groceries. "Help me, Neddy," he called out. Ned grabbed a sack of potatoes. "Heavens! I nearly ran down a wretched cat at the foot of the driveway. I think we're in for a big storm."

It was nearly as dark as night. Papa hurried into the kitchen and Ned watched him put away the groceries quickly, almost nervously, the way he did things he didn't like doing. Ned had seen him sweep up like that, and cook supper, nearly leaping from table to stove until his task was over. He was so different in church, stately and slow, moving from moment to moment, as dignified as the organ music that rose like a fountain from the pipes behind the altar, its calm voice untroubled by the quivering, uncertain voices of the choir.

"May I turn on a light, Reverend?" asked Mrs. Scallop, who had slipped into the kitchen. It was always dark in there except for a brief moment in the late afternoon when a ray of sunlight entered the kitchen window and lay like a cloth of gold across the worn oilcloth of the kitchen table.

"Of course, Mrs. Scallop," Papa said. "You don't need my permission, you know."

"Well—I'm thoughtful, Reverend," said Mrs. Scallop. Ned didn't think he'd ever met anyone who said so many nice things about herself. Mrs. Scallop held out his glass of milk to him.

"Was the cat gray, Papa?" Ned asked.

"I didn't notice, Neddy. Did you have a good day at school?"

"All right," said Ned. He took the glass and thanked Mrs. Scallop and turned away from her to drink the milk. He didn't much like her to watch him eat. She went off to the pantry and Ned felt that relief that usually followed Mrs. Scallop's departure from his vicinity. Papa washed his hands at the kitchen sink and dried them and sat down on one of the tall ladder-back chairs at the table. "Thank heavens I put up those lightning rods," he said, looking out the window at the black clouds in the sky.

"You know Billy? He tried to take the fangs out of a snake," Ned reported.

Papa made a grimace.

"And Janet Hoffman stopped him. She got him right down on the ground."

"Are you sure he was trying to defang it? I don't believe there are poisonous snakes around here."

"I don't know, Papa. But Billy was trying to hurt the snake."

"I expect he didn't know he might. Perhaps he doesn't understand a snake can feel pain."

"But he did!" exclaimed Ned. "Everybody does!"

"Well, this storm will clear everything up. We'll have real fall weather, a touch of frost . . ."

Ned leaned against a chair, feeling sleepy. "The snakes will sleep all winter," he said softly, "in their rocky palaces."

His father smiled and reached across the table and clasped his hand.

"I like the things you say, Ned," Papa remarked.

Ned felt for a moment the way he had last July 4th when he'd slid into the lake where Papa had taken him for a swim before the Waterville Fourth of July Parade, and the water hadn't been too warm or too cold, and he'd discovered he could swim nearly as fast as a waterbug. Or the way he'd felt one evening when he'd been sitting on the porch after supper, reading, and Papa had surprised him with a china dish full of peach ice cream he'd churned up himself with fresh peaches and thick cream. Papa had sat on the step while Ned ate, and Ned looked at his profile, sharp and clear like a profile on a coin you brought to a shine by rubbing it on a carpet. The twilight had been so soft after the heat of the day, and the air had been full of the scent of peaches.

Then Ned shuddered.

"You can hurt an animal by accident, can't you?"

"Indeed, you can, Ned. I've run over a nation of possums, I'm afraid. They're blinded by the head-lamps of the car, and I always see them too late."

"That's a relief," Ned said. Papa laughed. He knew Ned was imitating him. He often said, *that's a relief*, when the roof didn't leak during a rainfall, or when the well filled up with especially fine-tasting water or when he felt he'd preached a good sermon.

When Ned left the kitchen to go upstairs and do his homework, he didn't feel so lighthearted. A thought had slid into his mind: what if you *half-knew* you were hurting something that was alive? And how could you only half-know something?

Mrs. Scallop passed him on the stairs, whispering, "Lamb chops tonight."

The rain began, and fell steady and hard for hours and then, from up the river, came a sound like a distant cannon. By that time, Ned was in bed, reading about Robin Hood outwitting the Sheriff of Nottingham. The cannon drew closer, the claps of thunder louder. Lightning struck. It sounded so near that Ned knew it would soon be time to go down to the central hall. Ever since he could remember, Papa had come to get him during the storms that raged in the valley. No matter what time it was, when Ned heard the immense, rending sound of lightning striking the earth, he knew Papa would soon be at his door, saying, "Quick, Ned. Come downstairs. Hurry! Pull a sweater over your pajamas."

Ned understood that they had to be downstairs near the front door in case the house was struck and caught on fire. Papa didn't quite trust the new lightning rods. No sooner had that thought crossed his mind than his father's voice called out, "Ned!"

He ran out into the hall. As he passed his study, he heard the violent tapping of the maple branches against the window. Papa was carrying his mother toward the head of the stairs. The blanket he had wrapped her in trailed on the floor and Ned grabbed up its edge so his father wouldn't trip over it. For an instant, as a flash of blue-white light came through the window at the landing, he saw himself and Papa and Mama in the pier glass. Her hair hung down across his father's arm; her long twisted fingers clung to Papa's old alpaca jacket. Papa's eyes were dark, mysterious patches. His own face was a glimmer of white, his bare foot a splash of white floating just above the floor. Then the dark came back and they all vanished.

He heard Mrs. Scallop clumping down the back stairs. Mama's wheelchair was already near the front door. Papa had lit the kerosene lamp and placed it on a table that stood below the large painting of the Hudson Valley that showed how it had looked before all the villages and towns had grown up along the river, even before West Point had been established. The painting was filled with sunlight and with silence.

Mrs. Scallop appeared at the kitchen door dragging a chair. "I don't want to be in anyone's way," she announced, and Papa said, "Sit anywhere you like," as he arranged the blanket over Mama's knees.

The wind blew, the thunder rumbled, lightning lit up the sky. Ned felt as if the house were heaving and the porch lifting up like a prow, as though the house had turned into a great ship tossed by waves. Yet he never felt so safe as he did, sitting with his mother and father, during such a storm, listening to his father count the seconds between the claps of thunder, hearing his mother recall other storms and how wild they had been.

"Pity the poor creatures outdoors on a night like this," said Mrs. Scallop. "I can't help thinking about them . . . not lucky like us with shelter, a roof over our heads."

"Quite right, Mrs. Scallop," Papa said absently.

But Mama said, "I don't know that I'd agree with you, Mrs. Scallop. I imagine it could be wonderful to be out on such a night, right in the middle of all that noise and rain, not crouching inside a stuffy room like scared mice."

Mrs. Scallop made no reply. Ned saw her cast a glance at his mother then look down at the scraps of cloth in her lap, which she was braiding together. She didn't seem to need light for the work she did.

For once, Ned was on her side. It wouldn't be wonderful to be outdoors if you'd lost your balance, and couldn't see.

It wouldn't be wonderful, he thought, to be out in a storm if you were a one-eyed cat.

IV

The Cat

THE STORM SWEPT AWAY THE LAST OF THE SUMMER. Within a week of it, the tawny meadow grasses had grown dun colored and the trees stood black and bare as bones against the blue sky. One morning it was so chilly, the children could see their breaths, ghostly vapor that disappeared almost at once, and that made Evelyn laugh and cry out, "Look! Look, when I breathe!"

When Janet emerged from her path to join the others on their way to school, she announced that her cat had had kittens. "Their tiny eyes are closed and they could fit right inside your hand except you can't hold them yet, and they're so sweet!" she said.

Billy let out a whoop. "Itty-bitty kitty!" he bellowed, and smacked one hand against the other, then made two guns with his index fingers. "Boom! Boom! That's what I'd do to itty-bitty kitties!" he shouted.

"One has a patch over her eye," Janet said. "Just like a little pirate. That's what I'm calling her—Pirate."

"You can't call a she-cat Pirate," scoffed Billy. Janet completely ignored him.

"Do you know the woods are full of wild cats?" Ned asked.

"I wouldn't be surprised," Evelyn said, absently pulling at a piece of wool in her thick brown sweater.

"You'll unravel yourself," Janet warned her.

Evelyn's shoes were caked with dried mud and the hem was out of her dress. Janet was as neat as a new pine cone, but Evelyn looked like she was about to fall apart. They liked each other a good deal, Ned knew, and they often had peculiar dreamy conversations with each other that made no sense at all. Usually, Ned liked to listen to them, but since the night of the big storm the only subject which held interest for him was cats.

"You mean—you wouldn't be surprised because you've seen one?" he asked Evelyn.

"Six kittens," Janet said, "one right after the other. I saw them being born."

"Ugh!" exclaimed Evelyn.

"If I saw a wild cat, I'd chase it until I treed it," cried Billy. "Then I'd get a stick or something, or a stone, and I'd go—*bang*!"

"Did you? Did you see one?" asked Ned.

"I think I did," Evelyn said, picking a tiny fragment of eggshell out of her hair. "Now look at that!" she exclaimed. "I wonder where it ever came from."

"The cat," Ned reminded her. "Tell me about the cat."

"At nightfall," she said. "Probably after a chicken. I didn't pay much attention. I saw old Sport run right out to the end of his chain like a fish trying to get off the hook, and he was barking and I thought I saw a cat. But it could've been something else."

"Boom!" yelled Billy, racing past Janet. She clenched her fist and shook it at him. He giggled as if he was being tickled. She set off down the road after him, and Billy laughed so hard Ned thought he might fall down. People liked each other in strange ways, Ned had decided.

He turned to Evelyn, who trudged along beside him watching her own breath come and go.

"I wonder how they can live, the wild cats, I mean."

"They catch things, mice and like that," Evelyn replied. "They're good hunters."

"What if they're sick?"

"I *hate* writing poems!" Evelyn exclaimed. "Did Miss Jefferson give your class that assignment? To write a Thanksgiving poem?"

"What if a cat got hit by a branch?"

Evelyn punched him in the arm. "Stop talking about cats," she demanded. "You're as bad as Billy. I don't know nothing about cats. However, I know about chickens."

However was a word Evelyn had taken to using lately and she threw it in whenever she could.

"Was it gray? the cat you saw?"

"Ned Wallis!" she shouted.

"All right, all right . . ."

"Please give me an idea about the poem," she said in her usual voice.

"Write about pumpkins. Write about all the babies in your family getting together and chasing a turkey through the forest."

"You're making fun of me however," she said.

"Evelyn, will you tell me if you see the cat again? I think I might know that cat."

They had reached the state road. He saw Billy and Janet already entering the yard next to the red brick school.

"I might," said Evelyn and raced ahead of him. He stood alone for a few minutes worrying about the hours ahead of him, wondering how he would be able to concentrate on his lessons. "Concentrate," Miss Jefferson was always saying to him. What he would have liked to do was go back up the dirt road to the stone house and open a window and climb in and wander through the rooms. He sighed and began crossing the road slowly until he heard the second bell ring. Then he ran the rest of the way to school.

"Do birds ever drown in the rain?" he asked Mr. Scully one day.

"I don't believe so."

Ned thought he didn't sound sure. "What about raccoons? Can they drown?"

"I never heard of that," said Mr. Scully. "You have to remember you're talking about wild creatures. They have their ways—although they live and die just like all of us do."

"What about the cats you told me about? In the woods?"

"I don't recall that. But if you say so, I must have told you. My memory isn't a bit reliable. This morning, Ned, long before you were up, I was standing here just staring at my old wood stove. I simply couldn't remember how to go about making a fire. After a long while, the memory came back—as you can see."

A line of red outlined the door of the stove, and the griddle plate on top of it glowed with the heat. It was a good fire, Ned knew; it had been ripening all day long. Mr. Scully would keep the parlor door closed for most of the winter to conserve heat, he'd told Ned. But he didn't mind that, he'd said. As he got older, he liked smaller and smaller spaces.

"I used to have a dog," the old man said, rubbing his hands together. "I've had cats, too, but I was more partial to doggies. He was called Malthus. Of course, when Doris was little, we had puppies now and then, and she liked them, but it was Malthus I loved. By then, Doris was all grown up. I learned how nice it is to watch an animal instead of pouncing on it and hugging it every minute, covering up its nature with your own. Malthus liked cats a great deal. He'd wag his tail as soon as he saw one. There was something pleasing to me about that . . . a great big dog amused by a creature so different from itself."

"Like Billy and Janet," murmured Ned.

"I guess so," said the old man. Ned knew he hadn't

understood but he didn't mind. That happened a lot lately, and Ned had concluded that he and Mr. Scully were each telling themselves different stories like two people traveling along different roads. Every now and then their roads crossed.

Mr. Scully poured out their tea, then added a few drops of rum to his from his little bottle. He stared down at his cup broodingly. Ned guessed he was thinking about Doris so far away across the whole country. He'd brought Mr. Scully a post card from his mailbox this afternoon. It was from Doris. It was a picture of the Cascade Mountains, the same card she'd already sent her father three times.

"I'd better go get some more wood in," Ned said.

"I can tell by the draft there's a cold, cold wind," said Mr. Scully with a touch of sadness. "All right, Ned. Bring in some wood." He closed his eyes and leaned back in his rocking chair that had a faded quilted cushion Mrs. Scully had made years before. Ned knew she'd made it because Mr. Scully had told him so. It was the first time he'd ever referred to his wife. The only other thing Ned knew about her was that she had died when Doris was still a young girl. Papa had told him that, saying Mrs. Scully had been a very silent woman.

The yard looked much worse than it had in the

hot weather when everything had been green and underbrush had covered the rusting tools, and wild honeysuckle had drifted across the roofs of the shed and the outhouse.

The old quilt on top of the icebox was still damp from the big storm. Ned touched the lumps of quilt stuffing which looked like leftover oatmeal. He ducked inside the shed and at once heard a scrabbling sound. Out from behind a pile of kindling streaked a cat, its belly close to the ground. Ned's heart pounded. He ran out from the shed. The cat was already down by the outhouse looking back to where Ned was standing. It was the cat with one eye. It shook its head several times and sniffed the air, then it trotted off down the hill toward the state road.

Ned saw a bowl half filled with bread crusts on the ground. The cat must have been eating when he'd startled it by coming into the shed. He grabbed up an armful of wood and returned to the kitchen.

"Have you been feeding the gray cat?" he asked Mr. Scully.

"I do when I think of it," replied Mr. Scully. "Ned, can you see where I left my specs and the newspaper. The minute I put a thing down . . ."

Ned found the paper and Mr. Scully's spectacles on the seat of the chair on the other side of the table where he had dropped them earlier. He placed them on the old man's lap.

"Does the cat come to your yard a lot?"

"Indeed he does. In fact, he's been sleeping on top of the icebox. Otherwise I'd have gotten rid of that nasty old quilt. I caught a pretty close glimpse of him last Saturday. He looks a touch better. The blood is all gone. I'm pretty sure the poor thing is deaf though. I was nearly on top of him before he saw me, then he run off. He knows to come here for food now. That's something, I'd say."

Ned shivered.

"Want some more tea, Ned? You look chilled through and through. Another winter. Oh, dear. I used to love the cold so. Now I dread it. Nothing stays the same for long in this life."

On the way home up the hill, Ned paused to examine the new ditches which had formed since the storm. They would drive Papa wild, and he would exclaim, "I could fly to Jericho!" as the Packard bumped its way over the freshly destroyed drive. It was like a river bed; there were beautiful stones everywhere which had been exposed by the freshets of rain water. He looked up at the house. For a moment, he felt it was closed against him. He saw the car in its usual place. It was difficult to visualize the hill when the fields were bright with grass and sunlight and wild-flowers. It was hard to imagine the great lilac bush next to the porch in bloom, or the summer river so different from the dark stream that wound among the hills, bare now except for the patches of ever-green trees.

He didn't look up at the attic. It used to be the first thing he raised his eyes to see on his way up the drive. He would think about all the trunks and boxes he hadn't looked through yet, the books and magazines he hadn't opened. He had liked its unfin-ished look, the places where he had to be careful not to step because the boards were loose and he could see the original lathes and plaster the house had been made from. He had liked the small dusty windows, the narrow stairs he climbed. Because the gun was there in its case, he didn't care to think about the attic anymore. When there was a splinter in his foot, it was all he could think about; he would forget that every part of his body except where the splinter was felt fine. That's the way it was now with the attic. The gun was like a splinter in his mind.

He was relieved the old man was feeding the cat. He was worried, though, about Mr. Scully's mem-ory. He hadn't ever wondered about what cats ate. Perhaps if a cat was hungry enough, it would eat anything. He made up his mind to save scraps for it and drop them off at Mr. Scully's. A cat would like meat, he guessed, and Mr. Scully hardly ever had meat to eat. He lived on applesauce, and the soups he made from vegetables, and oatmeal, and the dark brown bread he made once every two weeks, round loaves of bread that tasted the way hay smelled. It was getting hard for him to chew, he'd told Ned, and then there was that memory trouble—he'd forgotten to put yeast in the last batch of dough he'd made and had to throw it all away.

Until Ned started doing chores for Mr. Scully, he hadn't realized people got old. He knew there were old people and young people and ones who were in between. But he'd not thought about people aging the way trees do, getting gnarled and dried out like the apple trees just above the stable that Papa said were too far gone to prune anymore.

Although the cat was so much on his mind, he found himself thinking often about Mr. Scully, especially at night when he felt the life of his own home gathered around him like a warm blanket, Mama reading a book in her wheelchair and Papa working on a sermon in the study—even Mrs. Scallop making one of her rugs. He would imagine David Scully in his dark little house lighting his kerosene lamps, though Doris had had electricity put in.

On the porch, near a loose shingle it might have

fallen from, Ned noticed a large, light brown husk of an insect. When he picked it up, it felt like tissue paper. Carrying it carefully in his hand, thinking to himself he might start a collection of dried bugs—they would be easier to get than foreign stamps—he walked inside and into Papa's study.

"How are you, Neddy?" asked Papa, who was sitting at his desk in front of his Remington typewriter. "Did you have a good day in school? How is Mr. Scully?"

Mrs. Scallop glided by the study doors, her nose in the air, looking as though she were about to sail out over the porch, the meadow, the monastery, and plummet into the Hudson River. Nearly at once, she passed by again on her way back to the kitchen. Ned knew she was reminding him that she was waiting in the kitchen with his afternoon treat—as she called it. He could also tell, in the glimpse he had had of her, that she was in one of her imperious, angry moods. He was getting used to them; it never occurred to him anymore to try to find out what had made her cross.

"Mr. Scully says he's having trouble remembering things," Ned told his father, looking at the bug on his palm. "He got a post card from Doris today. She always sends the same picture."

He went to stand beside the desk, keeping his palm steady. His father was staring at the sheet of paper in the typewriter; he didn't look to see what Ned was carrying, but he put his arm around his waist and gave him a small hug.

"It's hard to grow old and be alone," Papa said. "And then, of course, he has no church affiliation. That makes it worse. The church looks after her own."

"What about the others?" Ned asked. "Like Mr. Scully?"

"Don't worry!" Papa said cheerfully. "We'll keep an eye on him. I have a surprise for you." He turned to look at Ned. "What's that? Oh, a locust . . . The surprise is that Uncle Hilary has written about Christmas plans. He's been assigned to write a series of articles on historic American cities, and he'd like to take you to Charleston during your vacation. I've talked it over with your mother and we both think it's a fine idea."

Ned held the locust up and found that it was nearly transparent.

"Ned?"

"That's nice," Ned said.

"I'm surprised. You don't sound a bit enthusiastic."

"Can I go see Mama?"

His father turned back to his typewriter. "She's quite well today. Neddy," he said, and began to look through the notes piled up next to the machine. It was like Papa not to press him. Sometimes he was glad.

He walked softly through the hall, hoping he could get up the stairs before Mrs. Scallop heard him. But just as he put his foot on the first step, Mrs. Scallop stepped out from the shadowed corner beneath the staircase and turned on the little tulip lamp that sat next to the telephone. Its rosy light fell on her long apron and the tips of her brown shoes.

"A boy needs a snack after school, after all his work," she said.

He shrugged and went into the kitchen, where a plate full of hermit cookies and a glass of milk awaited him on the kitchen table. If he ate everything, Mrs. Scallop's mood might change. He knew by now that she enjoyed seeing people eat what she cooked. Ned put the locust down on the table. He suddenly imagined Mrs. Scallop stuffing the whole Wallis family so full of food that they would all float up into the sky, and she would gather the strings that held them to the earth and carry them around like a bunch of human balloons. This picture in his mind made him grin and he stole a quick glance at her. She was peering at the bug.

"Isn't that a locust?" she said. She touched it gingerly.

Ned was downing his milk as quickly as he could.

"I suppose you know how locust babies are born?" asked Mrs. Scallop in a challenging voice. Locust babies! Ned had to clench his jaw so as not to burst into laughter.

"It kills the mother, did you know that?" she went on. "They crawl out and the mother dies. That's the way it is with locusts. Of course, having a baby always costs a mother something. Like your mother."

Ned looked up, startled, his mouth full of hermit cookie.

"Oh, yes, my darling . . ." she said in a low voice. "It was after you were born that your mother came down with that terrible rheumatism!"

Ned gulped and choked for a minute, then cried, "It's not so! I remember when she could walk and run everywhere. And it's not rheumatism!"

Mrs. Scallop looked triumphant. "Some sickness takes a while to show," she said. Abruptly, she opened the cellar door next to the long sink and went down the stairs in the dark as though she were on an errand. He picked up the husk of the bug and put it on top of the cookie he hadn't eaten. Then he went quickly upstairs to his mother's room.

"I'm so glad to see you," she said, closing the

book she had been reading. "Isn't it amazing how dark it gets? It's not even five o'clock, yet it could be the dead of night." She held out her hand and he bent forward until his face was close to hers and she could kiss his cheek. He straightened up and stood silently.

"Ned—what is it?" She was staring at him very seriously.

He looked briefly over his shoulder. "Mrs. Scallop said—" he began, and then hesitated. His mother's attention at that moment bore down on him like the sun on a summer noonday; he would like to have hidden away in a cool shadow. "She said," he went on reluctantly, "that when locusts are born, the mother locust dies. She says that you got sick because I was born."

His mother looked so pained that he would have done anything not to have said those words. Desperately, he longed to tell her about the gray cat, about the shooting he had done at the stable. But how would *that* make her look?

He knew his mother hadn't gotten sick because of his birth—perhaps there was an inchworm of doubt stirring in his mind because of Mrs. Scallop's words, but that was all. He knew what he'd done, he'd pulled a false reason down like a window shade to hide the real reason he was unhappy these days.

"If I believed in witches——" his mother began. She shook her head. "No, she's not a witch. She's a bully, Ned. Papa keeps looking for someone else but no one wants to be out here, it's so far from town, and I don't blame them. I've often thought it would be the best thing for us to move to the parsonage, or maybe into Waterville. But your father loves this old house so. Ned, you know that isn't true, don't you? What Mrs. Scallop said? Your birth made me healthy. I felt so strong! I used to run upstairs and down, carrying you on my hip. One time, I climbed up into a tree with you. We sat on a big bough like two peculiar birds. I could have walked over the mountains. It was a long, long time before I got sick. Life has its surprises."

"I didn't believe her anyhow," Ned said. It was the nearest he could come to a larger truth.

"Papa has been looking very hard for someone to replace Mrs. Snort-and-Bellow——"

Ned burst into laughter. His mother grinned up at him. In that second she looked like her brother, Hilary.

"When you and Papa are gone, she comes up here and stands in the doorway and gabs away at me. I can't get rid of her. The funny thing is——she knows exactly what she's doing, and she knows I need to be by myself and quiet a lot of the time. She's taught me something, though. I used to think kind, humane people were the only ones to understand other people. It's not true at all. Mrs. Scallop understands . . . I think each person is a puzzle for her and, in time, she solves the puzzle."

"Does she know you're trying to find someone else?"

"Papa wants to find another kind of work for her first. We aren't just going to put her out."

"Wouldn't it be mean," Ned asked after a moment, "to give her to someone else?"

His mother laughed. "That's not what happens," she said. "Your Papa and I both know she would be very good in certain circumstances. What she needs is a small country of her own to run."

"Like the Red Queen," Ned said.

"Exactly," said Mama. "Now I have pleasant news. Uncle Hilary has written to you."

Ned started smiling. Uncle Hilary almost always wrote a note to him which was included in the letters he wrote to Mama. The notes were like small presents. One time, the whole note had been about a cat he and Martha, Ned's mother, had had when they were children. Martha, who was a few years older than her brother, had named the cat Aunt Pearlie, and for a long time, Uncle Hilary had thought the cat actually was his aunt.

Ned's mother lifted up the book she had been reading and handed him a note written on pale green paper. It said:

My Dear Nephew,

The subject today is friendship.

One time, after climbing an Alp, I slipped and broke my collarbone. Two days later, I came down with appendicitis. After I came home to my apartment from the hospital in Zurich (where I was living at the time), a dear old friend of mine drove 20 miles just to cook me a lunch of two boiled potatoes. To boil a potato properly is not as simple as you may think. It mustn't be soggy. It must be dry, floury. While I was reclining on my bed, happy to have escaped from doctors, my friend mashed the potatoes with a fork in a large white Swiss soup plate. He dotted them with butter, sprinkled them with a bit of salt and pepper. It was the most delicious meal I ever had. My friend, who is a painter, had given up his whole morning's work to drive to Zurich and make me my first meal after leaving the hospital. That is friendship. On the other hand, don't forget that you can have friends who do absolutely nothing for you or for anyone else. You like them for what they are. That's their gift. See you in Charleston, I hope. Love,

It was signed, *Uncle Hilary*. There was a postscript which read: *Driving 20 miles in Switzerland is no joke!*

Ned showed the note to his mother, and she smiled all the time she was reading it. It was the special smile she kept for her brother. Ned wished he had a sister or a brother, a person to whom he could confide that he didn't want to go away with Uncle Hilary; someone he could talk to about the gray cat and Mr. Scully's forgetfulness.

The real cold had not started. What would happen in December when the ground might be covered in deep snow? The cat would starve.

Ned had always loved Uncle Hilary's visits. They had been surprising, like mornings when he waked up and the ground was covered with snow which had fallen all night while he slept. He didn't want to think about Uncle Hilary now—or to imagine fields of snow.

If he could keep the cat alive, it wouldn't matter so much that he had disobeyed Papa, sneaked into the attic and taken out the gun. But if the cat disappeared, so that Ned wouldn't know if it was dead or alive, then his taking the gun would matter more than anything in the world.

"We'll miss you at Christmas, Neddy," Mama said. "But when I think of the fun you will have, I don't mind the thought of missing you."

100

Ned went and stood in front of the windows so he wouldn't have to answer. He didn't know what to say to his mother, any more than he had known what to say to his father about Uncle Hilary's invitation. Having to think so carefully before he spoke to his parents was terrible. It reminded him a bit of the time last spring he had neglected to memorize a poem, and when the teacher had called him up to the front of the classroom, he had had to stand there, saying nothing, feeling himself turn bright red, the children beginning to giggle, the teacher waiting, surprised, and then so disappointed in him.

"Maybe Uncle Hilary will have to go back to France," he burst out suddenly, turning toward his mother. "Before Christmas, I mean," he added, not looking at her.

"Oh—you needn't worry about that," she said. "I'm sure he won't have to go anywhere but where he wishes to go."

Ned felt miserable. He remembered a fairy tale Mama had read him about two children who had gotten bits of glass in their eyes, and how the glass had changed their vision of everything. He could sense that she was waiting for him to say something.

"I have to do ten long-division problems," he said, and walked quickly out of Mama's room. Another lie! And this one with the added flourish of a number!

That night, he thought he wouldn't get to sleep because of all the worrying he was doing about Christmas and Uncle Hilary.

He listened to the sighing of the wind outside his windows and looked out at the sky swept clean of clouds, so that he could see the glitter of the stars. He wondered if he was going to stay awake all night long. He began to recite to himself the names of presidents of the United States. Papa had taught them to him before he had started going to school. If *that* didn't put him to sleep, he made up his mind to get up, go downstairs and read all the newspapers on the library table. But he fell sound asleep just after he'd whispered, "Rutherford Birchard Hayes: 1877–1881."

When he woke up, the first thing he thought of was the cat. He dressed hurriedly, shivering. It was a cold morning, and he wished he could get back into the warm bed, into the nest of his own warmth, and hide his head beneath the pillow and sleep all day.

"Count your blessings," Mrs. Scallop ordered him in her loftiest voice as he sat eating his oatmeal. "You have been fortunate this morning. I didn't do to you what you did to me—leaving a dead bug on a cookie. What if I'd put it in your oatmeal?"

He dropped his spoon and ran out of the kitchen, hearing Mrs. Scallop announce to the kitchen table that he was a minister's son, and weren't they always the worst?

Papa was calling out goodbye to him, but Ned didn't answer. He grabbed his coat and books and fled from the house.

When he reached the end of the driveway, he paused and looked up at Mr. Scully's windows. The shades were drawn. No smoke came from the chimney. He imagined how chill the air was inside; he imagined the small old man lying beneath the thin blankets Ned had often made up his bed with. He went around to the back of the house. Nothing was stirring. Two crows flew past, black streaks against the pale morning sky. There was no sign of the cat.

He walked on down the road toward school wishing he'd meet up with Janet. Perhaps he would be able to speak to her about a strange thing that was happening to him. He had begun to fear animals, even those which he knew lived in other parts of the world.

Last week, as the children were passing the evergreen woods on their way home from school, a red-furred dog had rushed out from among the trees and made straight for Ned, barking and shaking its head from side to side like a pony. He'd fallen right down in the dirt and hidden his face until Billy, hollering and laughing, grabbed his hands and made him see that the dog was lying down next to him, licking the sleeve of his coat.

He had been looking through all the old *National Geographics*, too. He didn't go all the way into the attic but sat on the top step and reached out for the magazines, shuddering at pictures of anacondas and cheetahs, even of small creatures like flying squirrels and tarsiers. He'd asked Papa if there were poisonous snakes in the old stone wall that ran along the east side of the Wallis property where the sumac grew.

"Up in the mountains," Papa had said distractedly. "I don't believe they come down this low. Oh, perhaps the occasional copperhead."

Occasional copperhead! Ned had been horrified.

He saw ahead of him Janet skipping down her path to the dirt road, and he called out, "Wait up! Wait for me!" and she paused without turning around.

"Listen," he said when he'd reached her, "what do you think about Bear Mountain? Do you think there are bears there?"

"They put roads all the way to the top," Janet said. "When people arrive, animals go."

"All right, they go. But *where* do they go?"

"I never thought about that," Janet said.

"Are you afraid of bears?" he asked her with ef-fort.

"Well, I might be if one was standing on my foot. But I'm not scared of a bear that's maybe a hundred miles away."

Ned had been about to tell her that he was scared of the very idea of bears, but now he shut his mouth. He decided he'd better keep certain things to himself.

Mr. Scully was standing next to the pump looking out the kitchen window. The gray cat was close by the shed, eating from its bowl.

"He's getting a little plump," Mr. Scully noted. "I guess he's fond of the food I give him."

"Where do the wild cats go when it freezes at night?" Ned asked.

"I expect they have all kinds of spots for sleeping, a hole in a tree trunk, or an old chicken coop, or a hollow in the woods. Creatures like that get pretty clever about taking care of themselves. They have to do it every minute, I suppose, and that makes them alert and tough," Mr. Scully said.

"I wonder where he was born," Ned said.

"It might have been to a wild mother. Though he doesn't seem quite as timid as cats born in the wild. No—I think maybe he was a kitten of someone's pet, and he ran away or got lost, or else they put him out to fend for himself. People do that, you know." The old man suddenly leaned forward. "Ned! Look at that! He's playing!"

The cat was leaping in the air, chasing a leaf as it spun down from a maple tree.

"He's feeling better," said Mr. Scully.

Ned stretched over the counter and pressed his face against the window. As he watched the gray cat circle and leap and pounce, he felt light and hopeful; he felt free of an oppressive weight. Then he saw the emptiness of the cat's left eye which the lid half revealed. He saw the way the cat still shook its head from time to time as though something had crawled inside its ear.

Mr. Scully had gone to sit at the table. "He sleeps on that old quilt all the time," he said. The cat was sitting down near its bowl now, cleaning its thin little tail. Ned sat down with Mr. Scully. "I was going to throw the quilt out," the old man said, "but I'll leave it. The cat likes it so much. He probably feels it's his home. Another thing that happens when you get old—you wake up so early in the morning like you were going backwards through the night—and when I'm standing at the window, pumping water for my tea, I can hardly tell whether he's there or not . . . gray cat, gray quilt and gray autumn morning. It all seems one grayish haze. Then he lifts up his head and cocks it and stares at the window . . . looking to see if I'm up. He's getting to know my habits. Animals learn you, Ned, just as much as you learn them.

"Well, then he stretches front and back, and looks around and yawns and that's the first bit of color I see, that little pink spot of the inside of his mouth. He jumps down from the icebox and arches his back and runs about for a minute, disappears for maybe five or ten minutes. Pretty soon, when I'm drinking my tea, he turns up, ready for his breakfast. So I put something in his bowl and get my sweater off the hook and go out the back door and put the bowl down where he's used to it now, by the shed. He's less timid and lets me get a closer look, a little more every day or so.

"I close the door and come back to the window. He looks up at it, spots me with his good eye, then goes to the bowl and eats his breakfast. I do like to watch him clean himself. He licks a paw and runs it right over that empty socket. It don't seem to hurt him. After he's washed about every bit of himself, he struts off to do the day's business."

Mr. Scully's voice was so lively that Ned was surprised. He hadn't thought the old man was interested in much except the past, and whether or not he was going to get a letter from Doris.

"It's funny how alone an animal can be," Mr. Scully said in a musing tone, "and still be all right."

In the afternoon they sorted through boxes of buttons which had belonged to Mr. Scully's mother. "Just think how old these are," he remarked, some of the animation with which he'd spoken about the cat still in his voice, like the afterglow of a sunset. "How strange it is that the hands which formed them are long gone from the earth. How pretty they are! Look, this one is pearl—here's a bone button—this one is silver. It's a shame to throw them away, so much human thought went into them. What I'll do is take them to the Kimballs. With all those children, Mrs. Kimball can make good use of them. They don't have nearly enough buttons, I'm sure."

He poked Ned's arm and let out a cackle of laughter. "Now they'll have more buttons than clothes," he said. "Of course, Mr. Kimball is an independent sort of fellow, never wanted to work for anyone, so they struggle along. She used to be a practical nurse, I think. Imagine having so many children . . ."

"Evelyn is pretty nice," Ned said.

"I can't tell them apart," Mr. Scully said, looking cranky. "My wife never much cared for them. She was very particular."

"What does it mean—if you're particular?" Ned asked.

"It means you don't like much," Mr. Scully said gruffly.

It was time to go, Ned thought. The newspaper was folded on a chair, the floor swept, the wood piled up near the stove, handy for Mr. Scully. The two of them had emptied out a big box today. There weren't many boxes left to go through. But there would always be more to do. There always was when you lived in an old house, Mr. Scully had told Ned.

"I'll be going," he said.

"Thank you, Ned," Mr. Scully said, looking at him with a kindly expression. He wasn't smiling, but there was a certain softness around his eyes as he gazed at him.

"When the snow comes, where will the cat go?" Ned asked him.

"Maybe you can shove that icebox a little further into the shed," replied Mr. Scully. "That'll keep the wind and snow off of him. Makes a kind of winter nest." He looked out the window. "If I'm still here . . ." he muttered.

"Where are you going?" asked Ned. His voice trembled a little.

"I'm not *planning* on going anywhere," said Mr. Scully sharply. "But it isn't up to me anymore. See this?" He held out his thin, bony hand. "Now watch . . ." He very slowly tried to ball up the hand into a fist, but he couldn't. "I don't know how much longer I can manage, Ned," he said.

His words alarmed Ned but there was nothing he could think of to say to them. He muttered that he'd go out and push the icebox further under the roof of the shed. Mr. Scully nodded absently at him.

Later, as he walked home up the hill, Ned thought of Mr. Scully's hand which wouldn't clench and of his mother's hands, so often twisted and balled up. He stooped and picked up handfuls of stones and flung them into the meadows on either side of the driveway, hoping Papa wasn't looking out of a window and seeing what he was doing. It was bad enough, thinking about hands that weren't strong and straight like his, but added to that was the worry about his report card in his back pocket. It said Ned hadn't been paying attention in class. His grades were lukewarm, not failing. Papa would be serious; he'd speak in that cemetery voice and remind Ned that school was his job and he must try to do it well.

The late afternoon was cold and hard like slate. It would be cold in church on Sunday. The Sunday school classes would be held close to the door of the furnace room. After their Bible stories, the little children would cut turkeys out of orange paper with blunt scissors and nibble on the corn candies left over from Halloween. Holidays had an orange tinge to them except for Christmas which was red and green.

It was one of the busiest times of the year for the Reverend Wallis. There would be a special Thanksgiving service, arrangements to be made for the delivering of food baskets to needy people in the valley—some of them never came to church but were given baskets anyway—and, at the end of November, a pageant would be presented showing scenes of historical events since the founding of the church. Ned was to play the part of a carpenter's assistant in a scene in which the first meeting house was razed to make way for the present church. After that would come Christmas time when the church, lit up every evening, was like a village, with people coming and going, committees meeting, presents for the children being wrapped in bright paper, choir practice, and the whole church filled with the forest smell of the great evergreen tree that would stand in the corner below the gallery.

The church ladies used to provide a good deal of Thanksgiving dinner for the Wallis family. Ned had liked driving home from Tyler with their food hampers on the back seat of the Packard, carrying them into the kitchen and opening them up. It was a little like opening Christmas presents. Papa had cooked the turkey. When it was all done and carved, Papa would carry Mama downstairs and place her in her wheelchair, which had been drawn up to the round oak table beneath the Tiffany-glass shade.

This year, Ned imagined, Mrs. Scallop would be rushing about the kitchen, glowing like a hot coal, making huge cakes and pies, mashing potatoes, basting the turkey, telling anyone who passed through what a wonderful cook she was.

Do bullies know they're bullies? Ned wondered. Do people know when they're boasting? He walked up the porch steps and, through the window, saw his father sitting at his desk. He was only half glad Papa was home.

"Here's my report card," he said when he went into the study.

Papa smiled and took it from his outstretched hand and looked at it for what seemed a night and a day.

"Ned, I don't believe you've been working very hard," he said at last in a solemn voice. "Marks aren't so important. The fine thing is to do your best. Neddy, this isn't your best. Is it?"

Ned shook his head. His father uncapped his fountain pen to sign the report card. In two minutes, this would be over. In a week, he would have forgotten it. In ten years—

"Ned?" his father inquired, looking up at him. "Have you something to say?" When Ned didn't answer, his father sighed. "I don't see quite how I can send my boy away for a splendid holiday with his uncle if he is indifferent to his work," he said, looking down at his desk.

Hope stirred in Ned's heart. But he could hardly tell Papa that. "I'll try to do better next month," he said, wondering if he could get his grades down so low that Papa wouldn't let him go to Charleston with Uncle Hilary. Papa was smiling now. "That's the spirit," he said.

Ned was disgusted with himself. Bullies might not know they were bullies, but a liar must know when he had lied. Ned did.

❧

As it turned out, Mrs. Scallop didn't cook the Thanksgiving turkey for the Wallis family. She asked for the day off and went to Cornwall, down near the Hudson, to spend the holiday with a cousin of her dead husband's who lived there. Mr. Scully had his turkey with the Kimball family, and Ned and his father fixed their Thanksgiving dinner together. The church ladies provided three pies: mince, pumpkin and sweet potato. When the table was spread, it looked to Ned as if there was enough food on it to feed all the Kimballs for a week.

Mama wore her silk dress that was the color of lilac blossoms. On one of her fingers was an amethyst ring, her favorite stone she had told Ned. She was able to wear the ring because her finger joints were hardly swollen today. When Papa said grace, he added special thanks for Mama being at the table with them. When Papa looked up from his prayer, he gazed across the table at Mama for a long time. His face looked young the way it had years ago when he used to play with Ned before bedtime, playing hide-and-seek with him and laughing even harder than Ned had when Ned found him.

Except for the dark trunks of trees, there was hardly any color outdoors, but at the table there was a feast of light: the bright food, the blue and white dishes which were used only on holidays, the reflected glow from the lamp shade around which the wild animals paraded.

The three of us, Ned thought, and for no reason at all, he suddenly saw the cat in his mind's eye, not smooth and motionless and perfect like the animals on the Tiffany shade, but scruffy and dirty and wounded.

His mother was saying that she was specially thankful today that Mrs. Scallop had gone to haunt another household, and Papa laughed but reminded her—as he always did—that Mrs. Scallop had her virtues. Mama said they really ought to think about moving into the parsonage. Ned saw her father make a face.

"It would make life easier, Jim," Mama said. "And if you dislike the parsonage so much, we could think about a house in Waterville. Just imagine! No more Mrs. Scallop, no more leaking roof, driveway up-keep, tree pruning, paying the farmer to mow the fields. And we'd be closer to the church by several miles, and you wouldn't be driven to distraction by your worries about me."

Papa was staring down at his coffee, stirring it slowly and thoroughly. Ned knew that Papa liked coffee more than he liked most food. He drank cups of it while he prepared his sermons. He looked up at Mama.

"We love the place so," he said quietly. "What would you do without your view? What would Ned do without the maple branch he swings on, and the meadows he can run through and the trees he can climb?"

"I think of all the burdens it would lift from you— moving away," Mama said.

"The lilac bush," murmured Papa. "I'd miss that. When I imagine my father sailing up the Hudson and seeing this hill . . . when I imagine strangers sitting in this room . . ."

"It would be hard," Mama said. "But we must try to think. Ned, what would you say to our moving?"

"You've spent your whole life here," Papa said to him.

"I know it," Ned said. "What would happen to Mr. Scully? Who would bring his mail to him? Or chop the wood?"

He was thinking to himself: who will take care of the cat?

"We wouldn't move for a long time," his mother said quickly. "It is only that we must begin to think seriously about it. Once Papa finds work for Mrs. Scallop—"

"—Ned," interrupted Papa. "Why are you making that heap of turkey bones and skin next to your plate?"

116

Ned started. He felt a blush spreading all over his face and neck.

"It's leftovers," he said, stammering slightly. "It's—" He stopped speaking. For, perhaps, the time it took for his heart to beat twice, he nearly told them everything. Their faces looked so gentle in the lemony light. They were looking at him so fondly.

"It's for Evelyn Kimball's dog, Sport, that they keep on a chain. I thought—the dog looks skinny and the Kimballs don't have much, so it gets only a few scraps. I thought I'd give it a treat—"

He closed his mouth. They smiled at him. He knew his father might even praise him for his charity. His father often spoke about charity as though it was a person he loved.

He felt his stomach sink the way it did when he had to go to the dentist to have a cavity filled.

It would take him three minutes to fetch the gun down from the attic. It was with the gun that his trouble had started. Yet the gun hardly seemed to matter now. It was as if he'd moved away, not to the parsonage next to the church, or to Waterville, but a thousand miles away from home. What did matter was that he had a strange new life his parents knew nothing about and one that he must continue to keep hidden from them. Each lie he told them made the secret bigger, and that meant even more lies. He didn't know how to stop.

He got up from the table hurriedly and gathered up some dishes to take to the kitchen, miserable and ashamed as he glanced at their faces and saw written there their pride in him.

V

The Strength of Life

NED LOVED SNOW, THE WHISPER WHEN HE WALKED
through it, a sound like candles being blown
out, the coming indoors out of it into the warmth,
and standing on the register in the big hall through
which the dusty, metal-smelling heat blew up, and
the going back out again, shivering, cold, stooping
and scooping up a handful to make a snowball,
packing it hard with wet mittens, hefting it, tossing
it as far as he could, and the runners of his sled
whispering across it as he sleighed down the slopes
which were smooth and glittering and hard, like great
jewels.

On the first of December, there was a heavy
snowfall. When Ned looked out of his window the
next morning, the river glowed like a snake made

out of light as it wound among the snow-covered mountains.

He ate breakfast hastily, too preoccupied to read the story on the cereal box. Mrs. Scallop was broody this morning and left him alone, her glance passing over him as it passed over the kitchen chairs.

On the porch, he paused to take deep breaths of air which tasted, he imagined, like water from the center of the ocean, then he waded into the snow, passing the Packard, its windows white and hidden, the crabapple tree with its weighted branches, down the long hill trying to guess if he was anywhere near the buried driveway. By the time he reached Mr. Scully's house, his galoshes were topped with snow and his feet were wet. Mr. Scully's shades were drawn; the house had a pinched look as though it felt the cold.

Ned went around to the back until he could see the shed. There were boot tracks in the snow leading to it and returning to the back door. He guessed the old man had taken in the cat's bowl; it was nowhere to be seen. You couldn't leave anything out in this weather, it would freeze. Mr. Scully had told him that finding water in the winter was a big problem for animals. Licking the snow or ice could make them sick.

Ned stared hard at the shed. Perhaps the cat was inside, squeezed in behind logs in a tight space where its own breath would keep it warm. He was going to be late to school if he didn't get a move on, but he kept looking hard all over the yard as though he could make the cat appear out of snow and gray sky. Twice, his glance passed over the icebox. The third time, he saw that the motionless mound on top of it was not only the quilt but the cat, joined into one shape by a dusting of snow.

Ned held his breath for a moment, then put his own feet in Mr. Scully's tracks and went toward the shed. The tracks had frozen and they crunched under Ned's weight, but the cat didn't raise its head. Ned halted a few feet away from it—but of course, he realized, it wouldn't hear him because of its deaf ear. He could have gone closer to it than he'd ever been but he had a sudden vision of the cat exploding into fear when it finally did hear him.

When he got back to the front of the house, he saw fresh footsteps on the road. He could tell it was the road because of the deep ditches which fell away to either side. He guessed they were Billy's tracks. It was odd to think that Billy, huffing and puffing, had gone past Mr. Scully's place, thinking his own thoughts, while he, Ned, only a few yards away, had been searching for the cat. He found Evelyn's tracks, too, and later on, Janet's, the smallest of all. He felt ghostly as if he'd been left alone on a white, silent globe.

Somewhere in the evergreen woods, snow must have slid off a bough, for he heard the loud plop, then the fainter sound of the bough springing up, relieved of the weight. He thought about the cat, visualizing how it had looked on the quilt. How still it had been! Why hadn't he gone right up to it, looked at it close, touched its fur? Why had it been so motionless—still as death, still as a dead vole he'd seen last summer in the grass near the well? He came to the snow-covered blacktop road upon which a few cars had left their ridged tire tracks. He had a strong impulse to turn back, to play hooky for the first time in his life. Mr. Scully, with his poor eyesight, might not spot the cat on top of the icebox, might not, then, set food out for it. Fretting and shivering, his feet numb, Ned went on to school.

He tried very hard to concentrate on his lessons, to watch Miss Jefferson's plump, even handwriting on the blackboard as she wrote out the lines from a poem by Thomas Gray that the class was to memorize that week, but try as he might, the image of the unmoving animal on the ragged old quilt persisted. Last week, on a rainy afternoon, the cat had looked at Ned, had cocked its head as though to see him better. Its one eye, narrowed, had reminded him of a grain of wheat.

"The curfew tolls the knell of parting day,
The lowing herd wind slowly o'er the lea . . ."

Ned read the lines several times before copying them down in his copybook. The words made no sense to him. It was this that had made his hours in school so hard ever since he and Mr. Scully had seen the cat last autumn, this drawing away of his attention from everything that was going on around him. He was either relieved because the cat was where he could see it or fearful because he didn't know where it was.

In the afternoon, on the way home, Ned got into a fight with Billy.

Janet stumbled over a hidden root as she turned up her path. She fell forward, dropping her books. Ned picked them up, brushed off the snow and handed them to her as she got to her feet.

"Goody-goody!" shouted Billy. "Mama's goody boy!"

Ned felt a fierce single impulse. His arm swung

out like a chain of lead, and he knocked Billy into the snow with a triumphant howl of joy. Janet's mouth fell open in astonishment.

It was the deep frozen end of late afternoon, and the snow had hardened. He and Billy rolled about on it, grabbing at each other's ears and faces.

"Stop that!" Evelyn shouted.

"Oh, you boys! How I hate boys!" cried Janet.

Ned and Billy got to their feet. Billy's knitted hat was still on. Ned found himself hating it for its silliness—it stood up so high on top of Billy's great round head. All at once, Billy stuck out his tongue. Ned burst into laughter, and in a moment Billy was laughing, too. Evelyn gave them a disgusted look and trudged on ahead, but Janet paused, looking puzzled, and asked Billy if he *liked* to be knocked down. He only grinned at her.

For the first time in a while, Ned felt like himself, or what he thought of as himself. He and Billy walked along companionably all the way to Mr. Scully's house, talking about hockey, and how the pond near school must be frozen solid by now, and maybe the bigger boys would let them skate around the edges of the game this year. Ned remembered how the boys had skated, holding their hockey sticks diagonally across themselves, how their racing skates flashed

124

against the cracked, milky ice, how they'd shouted at Billy and him to stay out of their way, how they'd looked like warriors.

Billy went on home and Ned slid most of the way down to the state road to Mr. Scully's mailbox. There was no newspaper today; he guessed the snow must have stopped the delivery boy. But there was a handwritten note that said the new garage down the state road would be finished pretty soon. Mr. Scully's Ford flivver was practically buried by the snow. Ned guessed Papa would pick up Mr. Scully's groceries for him, just as he'd done in the past when the weather was bad and Mr. Scully was afraid the flivver would get stuck in a ditch somewhere.

His chin was freezing; he held his mitten over it, thinking how good a cup of hot tea would taste as he clambered up toward the house. He pulled himself over a patch of ice by grabbing onto the shingles of the outhouse. He looked over at the icebox just under the shed roof. The cat was lying on the quilt just as he had last seen it in the morning. He groaned out loud. He glanced toward the house. Mr. Scully was staring out the kitchen window at the cat.

Ned ran, stumbling and slipping, to the back door. Mr. Scully took a hundred years to open it.

"Is he dead? Is the cat dead?" cried Ned.

"Come in. Come inside, quick! Don't let the cold in."

Ned leaned against the kitchen table. The snow melted off his galoshes and made a little pool on the floor. He kept his eyes on Mr. Scully's face.

"Take your wet things off, Ned," the old man said quietly. "No, at least, he isn't dead yet. Right after you went home yesterday, I saw him scrabble up there on his quilt. He settled down and seemed all right. But when I set out his supper for him, he didn't pay attention like he usually does. It began to snow and I didn't know what to do. I didn't want to chance grabbing and putting him way inside the shed. Those wild ones can hurt you. And I thought maybe it would scare him if I tried that—he's such a timid fellow. I kept an eye on him and the snow got deeper and he didn't move. I went to bed finally. I told you how bad I sleep, Ned. Old people don't sleep the way young people do, they wake up so easy. Maybe it was the snow stopping that got me up. I came downstairs with my candle and set it down here on the table. I thought to have a cup of tea. Take off your coat, Ned. Put it over the chair there by the stove. One of the few nice things about age is you can give in to yourself in little ways. I wouldn't have dreamed of drinking a cup of tea in the middle of the night when I was young. Who ever heard of such a thing?"

Ned couldn't shake his head or smile or say a word.

"Calm down," Mr. Scully said. "The cat's sick. That's what I'm explaining to you. Anyhow, I looked out in the yard. I could just make him out, you know, because the sky was all cleared out of snow. So I put on my coat and my boots and went out to the icebox and stood right next to him. At first I thought he was dead, that he'd climbed up there to die. After a while, though, I heard him breathing, just a little whisper of air being taken in and let out. In fact, I even rested my hand on his neck and he let out a sound—poor devil, it wasn't purring—like a piece of glass scratching a stone. I guess his throat's hurt, too. I put his bowl of food right on the quilt beside him. He lifted his head a touch and looked at it out of his eye. But he didn't want it. His head sank down again so I brought the bowl back in. It would have frozen. Since then I've taken him food several times. He don't bother to even look now."

"Is he dying because of what happened to his eye?" Ned asked in a choked voice.

"I don't think that. People put out rat poison in their barns to kill the vermin. He might have eaten some. Anything can happen. Is that a letter in your hand?"

Ned handed him the notice about the new garage. "Pooh!" exclaimed the old man, crumpling it and putting it into the stove. Ned put his coat back on and walked out of the kitchen. Mr. Scully didn't say a word to stop him.

During the time he'd been inside the feeling of the day had changed. It now held the silence of midnight, a kind of silence Ned had listened to when he'd awakened with a sore throat, or a pain in his stomach from eating too much dessert.

He walked to the icebox, stamping heavily on the snow as he went. The cat didn't move. Ned drew closer. He gripped the icebox and peered up at the cat. He stretched one hand over its back. The closer he lowered his hand to it, the more he felt it was alive, even if it was barely alive. There was a breath of difference; he seemed to feel it in his fingers.

"You could tell, couldn't you?" asked Mr. Scully when Ned returned to the kitchen. "It's funny but you can always tell."

"He'll freeze to death," Ned said.

"You can't know that for sure. If the temperature doesn't drop too much further, he might make it. I'd let him come in here, but he won't do it. I've held the door open for him. He runs away."

128

It was brave of Mr. Scully, Ned thought, to have offered the cat the shelter of the house.

"Well, yes," the old man said, as though Ned had actually remarked on his bravery. "I did try—thinking about the hard weather coming up and him being in poor shape for hunting. But he seemed to be getting so strong. Ever since we watched him playing, I believed he might have a real chance. Here's your tea. Let's sit by the stove. Then I'd appreciate it if you'd fetch down one last box from the attic. I know it's there because it's not in the parlor. Once we've gone through it, the whole place will be in order. In as much order as I can manage."

Ned drank his tea. It warmed him and comforted him; for a little while he stopped thinking about the gray mound on the quilt. He went up a little ladder to the hole that let him into the attic and found the last object it held. It wasn't a box but a leather satchel, one strap holding it together, the leather nearly rotted away. There was nothing left in the dark space but cobwebs and old planks with rusty nails poking through them.

He brought the satchel to the kitchen table, and Mr. Scully unbuckled the strap carefully.

"Look at that . . ." he said wonderingly. The satchel was filled with a child's clothing. A blackened spoon with a curved handle fell on the table. The old man rubbed it with his finger and the tarnish came off. "Silver," he said softly. "What Doris ate her cereal with . . ." There were high-buttoned shoes that had once been white and were now the color of curds. Mr. Scully held up a sprigged cotton dress with a crocheted collar that crumbled in his hand. "She wore that to a birthday party when we lived in Poughkeepsie. My, my . . . think of her, way out in the golden west." He stared at Ned for a minute, then shook his head as though saying *no* to something. "I must throw this all away. There's no use for it now."

Ned washed their cups and piled up a few sticks of wood near the stove. He put on his coat. Mr. Scully said, "Ned, wait . . ." Ned paused at the door. Mr. Scully stared at him. Then he said, "While you were up in the attic, I looked at the cat. I'm pretty sure he lifted up his head."

As Ned walked home the dark set in. He was cold and tired, and fear for the cat's life tugged at him. Then he saw the lights shining through the windows of his home; he thought of the voices of his parents, and the echo of their voices that seemed to fill the rooms and halls of the house even when they were silent, Papa working in his study and Mama reading in her wheelchair.

He glanced through the bay windows of the living room and saw the pussywillow wallpaper his grandmother had chosen, the top of the bronze lion's back, the parchment shade of the lamp his father read the newspaper by. The room was empty. For a brief moment, he felt years had passed since he'd left for school that morning. He ran quickly to the front and up the porch steps, opened the door with a wrench and ran into the hall.

His father's coat hung from the coat stand, its hem falling on the handles of two umbrellas no one ever used. On the table where his father often left his old leather briefcase—and sometimes a box of chocolates he bought in Waterville—he saw an envelope addressed to him. It was the first letter Uncle Hilary had ever mailed directly to him. He opened it and read it:

Dear Ned,

On our way south, we may stop off to visit an island I've recently learned about where there are small wild ponies which live in a forest. Presumably, a ferryboat delivers mail and supplies to the island, so we'll just grab a ride on it. Be sure to pack books. I'll telephone from New York City as soon as I've made all our arrangements. I am only

131

sorry you don't have a year's vacation instead of ten days. But, of course, a person only has a year's vacation before the age of five.

Ned realized with a start that Christmas was only a few weeks away. He was standing there with his coat still on, wondering what could save him from this vacation trip which he now dreaded nearly as much as if it were to be spent alone with Mrs. Scallop, when she appeared, her finger to her lips, walking toward him. Since he rarely said more than hello to her, he couldn't imagine why she was warning him to be silent.

"You must be very quiet," she said in a loud whisper. "Your mother is very ill."

Ned tore off his coat, flung it at the coat stand and started for the stairs.

As he put his foot on the first step, he heard a trembling sigh that was nearly a word float down from above. He stopped, frightened. He turned hesitantly to Mrs. Scallop. She was nodding as though satisfied.

Then he took the stairs two at a time, going up fast because he didn't want to go up at all. He heard a second sigh, somewhat fainter. He reached the top of the stairs and saw his father bending over his mother's bed. His father looked up, saw him, and glanced down at the bed, then walked quickly out of the room to Ned.

"She's been suffering," Papa said in a low voice. "The pain has diminished, but she's quite weak. You'd best not go in right now, Neddy. You go and have your supper. I'll sit with her until she falls asleep."

Ned ate at the kitchen table, watched over closely by Mrs. Scallop, whose lips moved faintly each time he picked up a pea with his fork. She had made chocolate pudding, which was nearly his favorite dessert. He took no pleasure in it, his mind either on his mother or the cat. Mrs. Scallop noticed he wasn't eating and said, "Mrs. Scallop is known for her chocolate pudding, yet Neddy is so ungrateful for such a great treat that he simply fiddles with that wonderful pudding on his spoon!"

"What do you care whether I eat or not?" he suddenly cried out at her.

He had never spoken back to any grown-up before, and he was astonished at himself. Mrs. Scallop stared at him, her thin lower lip pushed out like a child pouting. "How could you raise your voice to me?" she asked in a tiny voice, as though her throat had shrunk to the size of a pin. To Ned's dismay, a large tear appeared on the lower lid of her right eye.

One tear, he observed to himself, despite his embarrassment—how can a person cry one tear from one eye?

He got up so hurriedly, he knocked the chair down. Picking it up, he muttered an apology. She hadn't moved. The tear traveled slowly down her large cheek. He had to go right upstairs to do his homework, he said, and he wasn't hungry tonight but he thanked her for the pudding. He was gripping the back of the chair so hard he heard the wood creak.

"Well, I *do* care what you eat," Mrs. Scallop said in a child's voice.

"Oh, I know you do," Ned said, and realized he had sounded just like Papa. Clumsily, half-bowing, he managed to get out of the kitchen.

At the top of the stairs, he saw a small lamp had been lit in his mother's room and placed near the windows. His father was asleep in the chair by the bed. Ned leaned around the doorway and saw Mama, her face white against the pillow, her eyes wide open. She turned her head slightly and stared up at him. She put a finger to her lips, as Mrs. Scallop had done, and pointed to Papa. She smiled faintly at him, and Ned tried to smile back.

He went to his own room. What a day it had been! The best part of it had been fighting, then making up, with Billy. He was almost happy when he shut the door and turned on the light and saw his books on their shelf, his yellow-painted dresser. He went and sat in the small woven chair Uncle Hilary had brought him from the Philippine Islands years ago. He could barely fit in it. For a long time, he sat in the chair and watched the lights twinkle across the river, glad to be away from the pain and craziness of grown-ups.

Later, when he crawled under his blanket, he found he couldn't sleep. He thought for a moment of taking one of his late-night walks through the house, but he suddenly recalled the rather strange emptiness of the livingroom when he'd looked through the windows after coming home from Mr. Scully's. It wasn't only that no one had been in the room. It was as though the whole house had been empty.

The cold didn't abate for several days, and Ned and Mr. Scully spent a good deal of time at the kitchen window watching the cat. It continued to raise its head now and then, and each time it did so, Ned and the old man would exclaim and one or the other would remark that it was still alive. They took turns taking out bowls of food. Once, Ned pushed the bowl right up to the cat's face and it made a sound. "It's like a rusty key turning in a lock," he reported to Mr. Scully.

"It wants to be let alone," Mr. Scully said resolutely. "And that's what we must do now, Ned, leave it alone."

"Couldn't we take him to a doctor?"

"I don't believe a doctor could get near him. Weak as he is, when I touched his head this afternoon before you got here, he hissed at me and opened his jaws. Let me tell you, Ned, he's a wild cat. We must wait and be patient and see. Anyhow, I haven't the money to pay an animal doctor."

The next day, Mr. Scully and Ned both concluded the cat was dead. There had been a brief snow flurry in the afternoon, and the animal was covered with a layer of snow. Mr. Scully had been unable to detect any breathing.

"Come away from the window, Ned. You'll wear a hole in the glass. If the cat's dead, I'll dispose of it tomorrow. I'm worried about a few things I want to talk to you about."

Reluctantly, Ned dragged himself from the window and sat down across from Mr. Scully at the kitchen table.

"It's the stovepipe," said the old man. His voice had risen and his skin had a mottled, bruised look. Ned realized he was agitated.

"There's a host of things that need doing," Mr. Scully went on, speaking quickly. "That stovepipe has to be cleaned out or I'll burn the house down around my head. I've written to Doris and I'd be obliged if you gave the letter to the Reverend and had him mail it. I'll give you the two pennies for the stamp. Winter is such a hard time! Just a few degrees difference in the temperature and look what happens!"

The old man's voice, its exasperated tone, showed Ned that he was tired of the cat. His heart sank. It was as if the cat weighed two hundred pounds and now he would have to carry it alone.

He took Mr. Scully's letter to Doris home with him and gave it to his father along with the two pennies for the stamp. When he went upstairs, he saw that his mother was dressed and in her wheelchair, for the first time since her attack on the day of his fight with Billy. She looked pale, but as soon as she saw him, she smiled and told him to come in. One of her hands was gripped around her favorite china cup that was painted with rosebuds and rose leaves and was so thin you could see through it when you held it up to a light.

"Don't look so worried, Neddy. I'm much better," she said.

He went to her, and she took her hand from the cup and put it on his. The swelling of her joints had lessened. He knew that that was what she had wanted him to see.

"It's mysterious," she said. "What makes it worse or better, no one seems to know. It's like sailing a small boat through reefs—you never know what you're going to hit or when. I'm tired, but that's all. I almost think I could walk. It's been a while since I tried. My legs are pretty weak, yet I think I could."

Slowly she extended one foot from beneath the blanket which covered her knees and lap.

"Uncle Hilary brought you those slippers from China," Ned said.

"He brings us the world, doesn't he? Aren't you glad to be going on a trip with him?"

It was hard to lie to her. Instead of answering her question, he said he had to run back to Mr. Scully's. He'd forgotten to bring in a second load of wood for the stove, and it was so cold, Mr. Scully might need it.

He ran downstairs and put on his coat and went outside to stand shivering under the crabapple tree on the north side of the house. As he looked up at the stained-glass window on the staircase landing, he knew he'd never been quite so miserable in his life. Through the kitchen window, he saw Mrs. Scallop standing at the sink. She seemed to be singing. Suddenly she flung out both her arms as though conducting an orchestra. She held a potato in one hand and a carrot in the other. In the middle of feeling so terrible, Ned found himself laughing. He could not have believed, until that moment, that Mrs. Scallop would ever be able to make him feel better—but she had.

He got up early the next day, Saturday, and started out for Mr. Scully's house without stopping for breakfast.

The weather had changed. The sky was clear, and Ned walked down the slope in the pale yellow winter sunlight. From the meadows rose the rustling sound of ice and snow thawing.

Ned stamped the snow from his boots and went into the kitchen. Mr. Scully was looking out the window. He turned to Ned, every tooth in his jaw visible as his mouth widened in an immense smile.

"He wasn't dead at all!" he shouted at Ned even though he was standing only a foot or two away from him. "The old fellow's gone! Look out there.

He got up and went. I can see his paw prints over there under the pine tree branch. See? Whatever it was—poison, germs—he wore it out! Now he's off to take care of things. He hung on. I'd given up—but he fooled me! Isn't that wonderful? To be fooled like that?"

Ned was dazed. Happiness came like a strong blow across his back, and it smelled of the fresh coffee Mr. Scully had made for himself and of wood smoke, and it was the buttery color of the ray of sun across the kitchen table, and the color, too, of the blackened quilt, no longer a bed for a dying animal.

He heard the Packard go by and wished he was sitting in it with Papa. He could have gone to church with him today after all, if he'd known about the cat. Papa would be meeting with the deacons about the Christmas programs, and the Ladies' Aid Society would be in the basement stringing cranberry and popcorn balls for the Christmas tree, and candying apples, and wrapping presents for the children of the congregation. And it might even be today that the great church doors would be opened and half a dozen men would carry in the enormous tree. One person would go up to the gallery and put the big star in place, then the rest of the tree would be decorated. And Christmas Eve the tree would fill the entire church with its marvelous smell of deep pine woods and snow, and there would be, too, the peppermint smell of candy canes. But he wouldn't be there! He would be on his way to Charleston with Uncle Hilary.

Mr. Scully was telling him that he felt so cheered up, he thought he'd smoke a bit of tobacco, although it had probably dried up by now and wouldn't be worth lighting. His pipe was in the parlor, and when he went to get it, opening the door wide, Ned smelled the cold apple-scented air. Mr. Scully kept his baskets of apples in the parlor, along with a sack each of potatoes and onions. Mr. Scully came back to the kitchen with his meerschaum, which had a collie dog carved in amber on the bowl. The old man looked stronger to Ned than he had for a long time, and he was moving quickly as he filled up the pipe bowl and tamped down the tobacco, got a match from the tin box on the windowsill, and struck it alight.

"He'll come back and I'll feed him," said Mr. Scully. "He'll be hungry now, and he'll want to get his strength back. Mrs. Kimball brought me a chicken yesterday. I'll give him some of that. You'll see . . . We'll have him running around soon."

"You're glad, too," Ned said, surprised. He had thought the old man was just being patient with him, putting up with Ned's concern about the cat. Now he could see Mr. Scully felt responsible—more than that, sympathetic—toward the animal.

"I'm glad," Mr. Scully said in a serious voice. "When you get to be my age, the strength of life in a living creature can't help but gladden your heart. I don't know the reason for that, but there it is."

Mrs. Scallop was somewhere upstairs when Ned got home so he was able to make his own breakfast and eat it alone in the kitchen. He washed his dishes and put them away, then he went upstairs to his mother's room.

"I am glad I'm going away with Uncle Hilary," he said to her.

She laughed, and said, "Why, yes! That is an answer to what I asked you yesterday, isn't it? Sometimes it takes you a while to answer a question."

He couldn't tell her all that had happened since yesterday, and why he felt so much better.

"I have some news. Your Papa has driven Mrs. Scallop to Waterville this morning. He's found work for her in a nursing home for old people. You remember how we talked about her needing a small country of her own? She may get one. Papa has taken her to her interview. She was wearing a hat that looked like a pumpkin pie. It may have been, for that matter. In any case, I'm sure it will impress the people who will hire her."

"How did Papa tell her that she wasn't to stay with us anymore?"

She laughed again. "We had to rehearse it all," she said. "He didn't want to lie, of course. But he had to dress up the truth a tiny bit. He hold her we were thinking seriously of moving to the parsonage, and that we really needed a practical nurse to watch over me until we moved. I'm so happy she's leaving." Mama sighed and looked out of her windows. "What a glorious day! I like that mildness that can come in the middle of winter. Well, she was efficient, I'll give her that. But I do believe she disliked me immensely because I didn't admire the heart on her sleeve enough. In fact, her real heart, I suspect, may look like one of those rugs she makes."

Ned felt Mama was really speaking to herself. She was still looking out the window; her voice was dreamy.

"Is there really going to be a practical nurse?" he asked.

She turned now and smiled at him as though suddenly seeing him standing there, his hand on the wheelchair arm.

"Yes, and it's Mrs. Kimball."

"Evelyn's mother?"

"Indeed, yes. The newest baby, Patrick, Junior, is on a bottle now, so that one of the other children can look after him. Your Papa spoke to her several weeks ago—it works out well for us all."

"Everything is happening," Ned said.

"It always is," said Mama.

VI

Christmas

MRS. SCALLOP, PAPA TOLD MAMA WITHIN NED'S HEAR-
ing, had filled the bill at the nursing home for
old people. Her interview had been entirely success-
ful; the owners of the home had been especially im-
pressed with her knowledge of how to make leftover
food appetizing, and also with the warm-hearted
feelings she said she held for old people. She would
be staying on with the Wallis family a few more
days before she took over her new post.

"There's that heart again," Mama said, grinning
at Ned.

"I hope you're not making fun of the poor thing,"
said Papa.

"An unfounded hope, Jim," Mama said tartly.

"I must admit, I won't mind her leaving," said
Papa.

Mrs. Scallop was more lofty than ever but it hardly bothered Ned. His confusion and apprehension of the last few months had sunk into the past, so that when he recalled some event, like the birth of Janet's kittens, for example, he would say to himself—that was during the time I was so scared and worried.

Then, in a minute or two on a cold afternoon, everything changed.

He and Billy had walked together from school to Mr. Scully's house. They had been speaking of all the things they liked best about Christmas. Billy said the absolutely best thing was not having to go to school.

Ned ran around to the back, stamped on the step to get the snow off his boots and opened the kitchen door. It was dead cold inside. No red line of fire outlined the stove grate. A few dirty dishes sat on the counter next to the pump. There was a box of oatmeal on the table, the cat's bowl, filled up with scraps of corn bread and bacon, and near the rocking chair, Mr. Scully's slippers.

Ned caught a blur of movement out the kitchen window. It was the cat walking across the snow to the shed. He lifted one paw suddenly and licked at it fiercely for a moment as though he'd gotten a piece of hard snow between his pads. Ned could see how

146

he was filling out, though he still looked pretty scrawny. Ned took the food and a saucer of water out to the shed. The cat watched him from several cautious feet away. Ned could tell how different the cat's attitude was from what it had been. It was guarded but not surprised by Ned's presence anymore.

He would like to have stayed to watch the cat eat, but he knew it wouldn't go near the bowl if he was standing so close to it. He went back to the kitchen and forgot the cat, trying to puzzle out where Mr. Scully was. He might have dropped in to visit Mrs. Kimball, although he'd often said all that yelping and sniffling and shrieking was a strain on him—babies crawling and climbing all over him as though he were the Rocky Mountains.

Ned saw that the rum bottle had spilled and leaked out all over the floor near the rocking chair. He looked toward the stairs and shuddered. The shudder was very strong and seemed to last a long time, and Ned wasn't sure whether it was from the chill in the house or from something else.

He slowly climbed the steps. Lying across the threshold of the bathroom Doris had paid for was Mr. Scully, face down, both arms stretched out in front of him, his hands clenched.

Ned ran all the way to the Kimballs' house. He banged on the door until it was opened by Evelyn's four-year-old brother, Terence. He was wearing an enormous gray sweater with holes in it, and one large fuzzy bedroom slipper. A horribly wet cookie was dissolving in one of his grubby hands. Ned looked past him into the large kitchen. Sitting near the stove was a small woman with a ball of white and black hair pinned to the top of her head. A baby was straddling one of her small knees.

"Neddy Wallis," she cried. "How nice to see you. Terence, go fetch Evelyn in the attic. See here, Ned, I've just made some Turkish Delight. Sit down wherever you can, and I'll give you some." As Ned gulped and started to speak, one of several cats prowling about the kitchen let out a wild yowl and jumped on another cat. The baby crowed with delight; Evelyn appeared and grabbed him up, shouting, "Hello, Ned."

"Mrs. Kimball," Ned said as loudly as he could. "Mr. Scully is lying on the floor of the bathroom in his house and he isn't moving at all."

"See to Patrick," Mrs. Kimball told Evelyn.

"I think he's dead!" cried Ned and burst into tears.

By then, Mrs. Kimball had thrown a man's heavy

plaid jacket over her shoulders and was sticking her bare feet into a pair of black rubber boots. The cats all ran into another room, Terence crawled under the table and Patrick laughed as if at the greatest joke in the world, his small hands gripping handfuls of Evelyn's shaggy hair.

Ned ran after Mrs. Kimball to Mr. Scully's house. She sprang into the kitchen and up the stairs, and by the time Ned had caught up with her, she was sitting on the floor and turning Mr. Scully over on his back as if he weighed no more than a pea pod. A pale line of foam had dried on the old man's mouth. Ned felt his stomach sink. Mrs. Kimball was holding Mr. Scully's wrist with two fingers.

"He's not dead," she said calmly. "He may have had a stroke. We don't have a telephone, Ned. Would you kindly go to your house and phone the Waterville hospital and have them send an ambulance here? Right away, Neddy. I'll make him as comfortable as I can while you do all that." She took Mr. Scully's flannel robe from a nail on the bathroom door and balled it up and pushed it gently under his head. "Hurry, Ned," she said.

He had never run up the hill so fast, he thought to himself as he gasped for air. He met his father in the hall just as he came out of his study.

"Papa, Mr. Scully had a stroke," he said. "Mrs. Kimball is there and says to call the hospital."

The Reverand Wallis made the telephone call, then told Ned he was going to Mr. Scully's to see if he could help. Ned had gotten over the sinking feeling in his stomach whenever he pictured Mr. Scully lying there on the floor, and he wanted to go too, but Papa said Ned had done enough for one day.

Ned watched his father's tall straight figure as he marched down the slope. For quite some time, there was no movement at Mr. Scully's. Then the ambulance bumped up, and two men got out of it carrying a stretcher. Pretty soon they returned carrying Mr. Scully beneath a bright red blanket. Ned could see Mrs. Kimball as she crossed the road on her way home. After the ambulance left, Papa stood alone for a minute looking at the little house. For Ned, it had all been like watching a pantomime.

What he hoped was that the cat wouldn't be frightened away for good by all the people coming and going. He hoped Mr. Scully would be all right, too, but it didn't seem a separate hope. It was as if Mr. Scully and the cat were one large, perplexing trouble. Just as he saw Papa start up the slope, he heard Mrs. Scallop clumping down the back stairs.

"What's the matter with you, Neddy, my darling

boy," she said, "you are all red in the face and your knees are quaking."

He opened his mouth and she said at once, before he could speak, "Calm down, calm down." He hated the way she spoke in that false soothing voice, as if she owned the country of calm and he was some kind of fool who'd stumbled across its borders. He waited a moment. It didn't seem to bother her—she was smiling at him as though she knew exactly what thoughts were in his head.

"Mr. Scully is sick," he said finally, and started to go out of the kitchen, thinking to himself how glad he was she was going away.

"I know all about that," she said sharply, "of course I do! Don't you think your Papa would tell me anything that important? In any case, I heard the telephone call he made. I've had experience with old people living alone—deserted by ungrateful children."

Ned went into the hall thinking that if Mrs. Scallop had Doris in mind when she spoke of ungrateful children, he couldn't help feeling sorry for Doris.

His mother seemed to be waiting for him. She was looking eagerly toward her doorway.

"I'm so sorry about Mr. Scully," she said. "I think you'd grown quite fond of him, hadn't you?"

"I thought he was dead," Ned said. "He looked dead."

She looked at him intently. "Was it you who found him? I thought it was Mrs. Kimball."

"I did. I went to see—" he paused. He had been about to say that he had gone down to see how the cat was faring. He began again. "I went to see him, see if he was all right." He felt an odd little stir of excitement that he was using "him" for both the cat and Mr. Scully, and that his mother couldn't guess what he was doing.

"You must have been so frightened," she said. "Seeing a person you know like that, lying so still on a floor. Oh—I know you must have been scared!"

"My stomach was scared," Ned acknowledged.

"You may have saved his life," Mama said.

Whose life? wondered Ned.

"When people have strokes, the faster a doctor gets to them the better chance they have."

He wished suddenly that he could go into his room and lock the door and not talk for a while, not even to his mother. He felt a painful confusion; the excitement he had felt a minute before was gone. He wished there was someone who could make him speak of the cat, a magician, perhaps, who would magically draw the words from him.

His mother was still looking at him closely.

"Can people die from a stroke?" he asked dully.

"Yes," she said. "It used to be called apoplexy, I think. The blood the brain needs gets blocked by something, and it can't reach the brain cells. A person's speech can be affected, or the movement of their right or left sides. Mr. Scully is quite elderly. Even if he recovers, Ned, he may not be the same."

"He won't be coming back to his house?" Ned asked.

"It isn't likely—unless there is someone to take care of him," she replied.

"But what will happen?" Ned cried out. "What will happen to his house?"

"His daughter will have to come and see to things. Oh, Ned, I didn't know you cared so much about him! There's nothing we can do now, only wait. By the time you get back from your trip with Uncle Hilary—"

"No!" exclaimed Ned. "I can't go anywhere with Uncle Hilary."

"Neddy, what is it?"

Mrs. Scallop entered the room noiselessly. "Ned, you will upset your poor mother with all this noise!"

"You, Mrs. Scallop, will please not speak for me," said Mrs. Wallis in such a stern voice that Ned forgot about himself for a moment. "I'm very thirsty," Mama continued, her voice softening only slightly. "And I feel a chill. Would you please bring me something hot to drink?"

When Mrs. Scallop had reluctantly left the room, Mrs. Wallis whispered to Ned, "I'm not chilled or thirsty, Neddy . . . You do look surprised!" She smiled at him and touched his chin. "I'm not good like your father. Sometimes I tell fibs." She took his hand then and pressed it in her own. "Ned, why can't you go with Uncle Hilary? A person shouldn't have to tell everything, but sometimes a thing gets in the way of a person's life. I feel as if something has happened to you."

He stared at her, feeling a desperate hope that she might guess it all. But would she still hold his hand the way she was holding it now if she knew he had shot away a cat's eye? Made something alive suffer? He'd brought her a field mouse once that he'd caught near the lilac bush, and she'd petted it with one swollen finger, her face wreathed in smiles, and she loved birds, and she'd loved her own cat, Aunt Pearlie.

But wouldn't she understand that he hadn't really known the shadow was alive?

"Oh—" she groaned suddenly. "If only I could move about!"

Had he known it was alive?

"I don't want to go to Charleston," he said, his voice trembling slightly. "I don't want to go away from home."

Mama stroked his hand.

"All right, Ned," she said in a very quiet voice. "You don't have to go. We'll get in touch with Uncle Hilary. I know he'll be sorry. But there'll be another time."

Mrs. Scallop left a couple of days later, wrapping her rugs up in thick cord and refusing to let anyone help her carry them to the Packard. She did not behave in the least put out by her leaving. She told Ned she was moving on to higher things. It had been hard on a woman as active as she was to be stuck out in the country. Now she'd be in the middle of town, with more people to talk with than a child and an invalid. She left a vast pile of rich chocolate brownies on the kitchen table. He made up his mind not to touch them but even as he did so, he found he had one in his hand.

After Papa had driven off with Mrs. Scallop, Ned went up the back stairs to her room. It was emptier, it seemed to him, than it had ever been, as though she had taken some invisible substance from it. The oak dresser was dusted, a thin white coverlet covered the mattress ticking. Mama said the house felt larger now that Mrs. Snort-and-Bellow had gone.

Mr. Scully would not be coming home for a while, Ned learned from Evelyn, who had heard the news from her mother. He had had a stroke; he couldn't speak or move his right arm and leg. Doris had been sent for and was coming East to see her father.

Every afternoon, Ned went to Mr. Scully's back yard and waited for the gray cat. When it was bitterly cold, he stayed inside the woodshed, holding the paper bag of leftovers he had collected against his body so the food wouldn't freeze. As soon as he saw the cat coming from behind the outhouse, Ned would fill up the old bowl and put it on the ground. The cat would approach the shed with great caution, its head cocked as it kept its eye on Ned. He would back into the shed until the cat appeared satisfied at the distance Ned was standing from the bowl.

When Ned saw him eating, Ned felt as though he himself were being filled up, and that as the cat's hunger was eased, Ned's thoughts were freed from it. When he was with the cat, he could be unmindful of it.

He couldn't carry milk to school and back to Mr. Scully's shed. One day Papa took him for a haircut to the barbershop on River Street in Waterville. Afterwards, Ned told his father that he'd like to go down to the wharf where the Hudson River Dayline boats stopped to pick up passengers or drop them off. He told Papa he'd like to go by himself. His father had looked faintly surprised but had said, "All right," and gone off to Schermerhorn's, the big department store in town, to buy Mrs. Wallis a bed jacket.

Ned went to a grocery store and bought several cans of evaporated milk with the money he had earned from Mr. Scully, then to the hardware store where he found a small ice pick. He was pretty sure his father wouldn't notice the bulging pockets of his coat. His father tended to look mostly at peoples' faces, not at what they were wearing.

When he got back into the Packard that day, his neck feeling cool and light after his haircut, he almost giggled because the cans of milk thudded noisily against each other as he settled into the seat. Papa didn't even look over at him.

"What do you do all the time behind that house," Billy asked him one afternoon after school.

"I'm cleaning up things for Mr. Scully," replied Ned without hesitation. "When he comes home from the hospital, the yard will be the way he wanted it."

"But there's snow over everything," Billy said.

"I'm working in the shed right now. There's lots to do there," Ned said.

He wondered if there was anything he couldn't lie about now. It seemed to him he didn't even care anymore.

A week after Mr. Scully was taken to the hospital, Ned found the old Waterville taxi parked in front of his house, and Mr. Grob, the ancient taxi-driver, sitting in the front seat and blowing on his hands to keep them warm. The flivver had sunk into the snow past its windows.

Ned went around to the shed. He had some pork scraps in his lunchbox from last night's supper. He emptied them into the bowl, then poured evaporated milk over them from the can he'd punched holes in with the ice pick.

"Boy!" said a loud voice.

He turned to look at the kitchen door. A woman in a very thick, brown coat was standing on the step.

"What are you doing there?" she demanded.

"I'm feeding the cat," he answered, too surprised

by the woman's presence to say anything but the truth.

"My father didn't have a cat," the woman said severely. "He would have told me if he had."

"I work for him," Ned said.

"He didn't have anyone working for him. He didn't need anyone," she said.

"I chopped wood and brought it in for him, and got the mail from down the hill—when there was any mail—and I kept him company," Ned said.

He felt a strange kind of exhilaration, a consciousness of strength as he stood there, talking to the resentful woman in the brown coat whom he knew was Mr. Scully's daughter, Doris. He realized suddenly that it had been a long time since he'd been able to give a true account of what he was doing and why he was doing it.

"Well, you won't be keeping him company anymore," she said.

He was afraid to ask her what she meant, although he was pretty sure his mother would have known, and would have told him, if Mr. Scully had died. He stared dumbly at her.

"He can't do for himself at all now," she said in a slightly less stern voice. "He can't speak. He certainly can't come back to this hovel."

Hovel! It was true Mr. Scully's house was small and old and a bit decrepit, but it had fit so nicely around him, like a shell around a snail. Ned wondered what Doris's idea of a house was.

"I'm going to try to sell it," she said. "He'll need every cent he can get for the nursing home."

"Isn't he in the hospital?"

"He'll be moved out of there pretty soon."

Ned had a powerful wish to see the old man, to watch him pouring out a drop of rum into his tea.

Now Mr. Scully's daughter drew up the collar of her coat, nearly hiding her face. She was staring across the valley to the low range of hills on the other side. "Snow!" she exclaimed scornfully. She turned her head and looked at Ned.

"Well, I guess you can feed the cat until someone buys this shack," she said.

"Could I see Mr. Scully?"

"I suppose so," she replied grudgingly. "Though it would be like visiting a wall, the way he is now. The doc says he might get better—you can't tell with that sort of thing. He can hear though. If you want me to tell him something . . ."

"Tell him I'm taking care of our cat," Ned said. Doris nodded without looking at him and withdrew into the house.

Whether it was Mr. Grob and his taxi, and Mr. Scully's daughter being in the house, or for some other reason, the cat didn't show up for a few days. Ned would empty out the nearly frozen food he'd left the day before and replace it with fresh food and milk. Now that Mrs. Scallop was no longer at home, keeping a watch on him with her little blue-dot eyes, he took whatever he thought the cat would eat. Mrs. Kimball was friendly and pleasant to him, but she didn't pay any attention to what he did in the kitchen or the pantry. He guessed she was pretty accustomed to children coming and going and poking about and doing things that mostly didn't concern or worry her.

Three days before Christmas, Ned found a sign on a post stuck into the ground in front of Mr. Scully's house. It said: "For Sale." There had been no Waterville newspaper in the mailbox for several days. As Ned started up the hill, he thought he glimpsed the cat a hundred yards or so away slipping behind a spruce tree. He didn't go after it, he figured it had been scared enough by the taxi and Doris. When he got to the shed, he was elated to find the bowl empty of the food he'd put in it before he went down the hill to the mailbox.

But his elation didn't last longer than two minutes.

He thought of the hard months ahead, January and February and March. How would he be able to keep the cat alive until the warmer weather came?

School, his classes, church, were like a faint mumble in another room. His conversations with Mama had become increasingly uneasy. He could see she was bewildered. Taking the gun from the attic and shooting it—his first disobedience—had happened years before, it seemed to Ned. All the lies he had told, the subterfuge, were piled up over the gun like a mountain of hard-packed snow. He felt his secret had frozen around him. He didn't know how to melt it.

Ned watched Papa take a long fur cape from a closet and unwrap the sheet that covered it. Mama's grandmother had left it to her in her will, and Mama always wore it on Christmas Eve when Papa drove them all to the church.

Ned drew his hand over the soft fur.

"What's it made of, Papa?" he asked timidly.

"I think it's seal," Papa answered.

He and Papa trimmed their own small Christmas tree that stood in the living room across from the library table. Ned's throat began to feel very sore.

"Neddy, you look so flushed!" said Papa. "Do you feel all right?"

"No," Ned said miserably.

A half hour later, Ned was in bed, his teeth chattering, as Papa piled up blankets over him.

He shivered or burned all the next day. "Mrs. Kimball will come and stay with you," Papa said. "And Mama is going to stay home, too. I know how disappointed you are, Neddy dear. But you mustn't go out as sick as you are."

He didn't care now about missing the sight of the great Christmas tree with all its lights turned on any more than he cared about the trip with Uncle Hilary. He imagined himself throwing off the blankets and running down the hill to take food to the bowl. But he really knew he couldn't, and wouldn't, do that.

In the past he had sometimes liked being sick. His father would bring him a tray with a tall glass full of eggnog on it, or dry, slightly cold toast that had a chewiness he liked, or milk toast, warm and comforting in a soup bowl. His mother would call out to him from her room, and tell him stories after Papa had wheeled her chair close to Ned's door.

But now he was frantic.

It's such an awful cat, he suddenly thought as his father stood beside his bed, waiting for the five minutes to be up when he could remove the thermometer from Ned's mouth. It was ugly and battered; its fur was patchy; its toes stuck up and its whiskers were sparse. It would never be like one of Janet's kitties that meowed sweetly and sat on her lap and purred. It had a black hole for an eye.

The eye. His fault! His father removed the thermometer from his mouth. Ned whispered, "Die, cat, die!"

His father bent over him and asked softly, "What, Neddy?"

Ned shook his head. His father placed his long cool hand on his forehead.

VII

Disappearances

NED'S FEVER DROPPED TO NORMAL THE DAY AFTER Christmas. Papa said he could get up as long as he kept himself warmly dressed and didn't come downstairs where the rooms were so drafty.

For the first time that he could recall, Ned wished school vacation was over. Each day was a week long. He went from window to window and stared out at the snow-covered landscape. In other seasons of the year, something moved or fluttered or flew past, leaves, birds, insects, squirrels—the meadows waving like banners in a breeze—but now nothing moved that Ned could see except for the tiny drops of moisture from his breath upon a windowpane.

He spent a few minutes with Mama each day. She wasn't feeling well either. Upstairs was like a hospital. Papa went up and down with trays of food and emptied dishes, smelling faintly of evergreen tree. Papa had put the silver icicles, one by one, on their own Christmas tree on Christmas morning, but Ned hadn't been down to see it yet. Everything was so separate, the tree, Papa, Mama, himself. His limbs were heavy; he could even feel the dullness of his own gaze. He moped around, occasionally galvanized by the explosion of a violent sneeze. His whole room smelled of cough medicine.

Wearing his old brown wool bathrobe which he'd long outgrown—the belt loops were practically up under his arms—he halfheartedly played with his Christmas presents. He learned to tap out the distress signal on the sender of the Morse code set Papa had given him, and to adjust the eyepiece of the microscope Uncle Hilary had mailed to him from New York City. It was secondhand, Uncle Hilary had written, but it was real, and he hoped Ned would get some enjoyment from it, although it was no way near as wonderful as a trip to Charleston would have been.

The only thing that really took his mind off the slow passage of the hours was *Kidnapped*. Each day after lunch, he read a few pages of it. But there were moments, even when he was reading, when he jumped up agitatedly and roamed through the rooms, thinking of Mr. Scully lying in a hospital bed, thinking about the cat, wondering if it could be alive in the frozen world outside the windows.

Finally the day came when he put his bathrobe away and dressed in outdoor clothes, when food tasted good to him for the first time in a while, and when he opened the front doors and gulped in a great draft of snowy air and started off to school. Ned half-forgot Mr. Scully and the gray cat.

The landscape didn't seem frozen anymore. He saw tracks in the snow, animal and human. Bare branches rattled, smoke rose out of chimneys, a small gray bird chirped on the branch of a pine tree and the sound of Evelyn's dog barking cracked the still air; the snow had its own noises, too; it shifted and thawed or hardened, it whispered or squeaked when he walked on it.

He was glad to walk home with Billy and Janet and Evelyn that day. It began to snow just as the four children went past the stone house. Ned was blinded by the great fast-falling flakes. Sometimes he listened to the sea in a large seashell Uncle Hilary had brought him from a Caribbean island. The heavy fall of snow muffled all sound; it made a kind of soft roaring, and Ned felt as if he'd been suddenly transported into that seashell.

One day followed another. The sun moved ever

higher across the sky, and although its light was pale, it felt different, warmer, heavier. He hardly ever went directly home after school.

He wandered about the hills. He took paths through deep woods he'd not ventured into before. He cut across fields where he sometimes sank up to his waist in snowdrifts. His favorite spot was the Makepeace estate. He would go up the hill, following the old stone wall which ran along the Kimball property, and he would laugh to see Sport charge out on his running line and look up at the sky, barking, as though Ned were floating around somewhere just above him.

When he emerged from the pines onto the crest of the hill where the abandoned mansion stood, he knew he'd found his way into the heart of winter. If he looked north, he could, if the sun was out, catch the glint of an attic window in his own house.

The snow was piled up around the base of each column. Ned sat on the edge of the wicker settee and gazed out at the mountain across the river. Although he was on the same crest on which his house had been built, the view was entirely different. While he sat there, he could feel how rapidly his heart was beating. It was as though he were waiting for something to happen, something unexpected that could be either terrible or wonderful.

One afternoon when the woods were spongy with melting snow and Ned was standing on the Makepeace veranda, his galoshes soaked through, he saw the flicker of something unusual at the edge of his vision, a blur of movement, quick and indeterminate, just where the meadow ended and the woods began. He stared at the spot where it had been as though he were looking through his microscope. It was the cat. Or *a* cat. Even as he looked, it disappeared like a puff of Mr. Scully's tobacco smoke caught in a draft. It had been holding something in its mouth.

He went to sit on the settee. Evelyn had said the whole place was haunted. Ned wasn't afraid. The mansion looked ancient to him, like the Greek temple he'd seen on one of his post cards. He hadn't felt any impulse to go after the cat. *That* haunted him a little; that was a mystery. If the animal he'd seen was the cat with one eye, it had managed to live a long time without his help, he told himself. He was immensely relieved that he hadn't been able to see it clearly. He didn't want to feel sorry for it anymore.

On his way home he stopped briefly at Mr. Scully's house. The "For Sale" sign was gone. The Ford flivver had disappeared and the outhouse had been taken down and its lumber stacked near the back door. Ned found the cat's bowl in the shed. He walked a few yards down the hill toward the state road carrying it. Suddenly, he raised his hand and flung the bowl with all his might. He turned and ran to his driveway, not looking back, not hearing when the bowl landed.

"Where have you been, my wandering boy?" his mother asked. Mrs. Kimball had just brought her a cup of tea. Mrs. Kimball didn't make treats the way Mrs. Scallop had. She wasn't a very good cook, but she was so kind and agreeable, Ned didn't mind. Mrs. Scallop was a person who could interfere with you by just glancing in your direction, but Mrs. Kimball, even when she was reminding you of something you ought to do, somehow let you alone.

"I've been going to the Makepeace mansion a lot," Ned said. He looked out of the bay windows and saw the Makepeace chimneys. In the summer, the line of maple trees would hide them from view. "What happened to them?" he asked. "Did you ever know them?"

"The family lived in this part of the Hudson Valley since the eighteenth century," she said. "Parts of that house are pre-Revolutionary."

"Evelyn says there are ghosts there."

His mother looked at him over her teacup. He felt he hadn't seen her for some time—though he visited her every day for at least a few minutes. Perhaps it was that he hadn't really looked at her for a while. She seemed more stooped. Her voice had thinned out, too.

"I don't think there are ghosts," Mama said slowly. "If it is haunted, it is only by the suffering of the people who lived there. They were still a large family when your grandfather bought our land. Three sons were killed in the World War. Two of the daughters married and moved far away from this part of the country. When I came here as a young bride, all that remained of the Makepeaces was a tiny old couple, nearly as small as the figures on a wedding cake. When they died, the eldest daughter took away all the furniture and closed up the house and put it up for sale. No one bought it. When I could still walk, I used to go over there and sit on an old wicker settee on the veranda. I took you there a few times, I think."

"That's where I sit now," Ned said.

"Do you?" she asked so gently that Ned had to look away. For some reason, his eyes filled with tears.

"It's not really haunted, Neddy," she said, more

firmly. "I think there are presences everywhere, the souls of all who have gone through this world."

"I thought they were in heaven."

"Yes, that's what Papa says."

Ned reached out and touched her hair for a second.

"The 'For Sale' sign in front of Mr. Scully's house is gone."

She told him that the house had been sold, and that Mr. Scully had been moved to the Waterville nursing home.

"Isn't that where Mrs. Scallop works?" he asked, startled.

"Yes, it is. But we needn't worry. She is, well, nicer may not be the right word, but calmer anyhow now that she is in charge of things. Papa went to see Mr. Scully and says Mrs. Scallop pays a lot of attention to him, and to every other patient in the place."

"Is Mr. Scully better?"

"He has some small movement on the side affected by the stroke, but he can't speak."

"Did his daughter stay here?"

"She went back to the West."

It didn't seem possible that only five months had passed since his birthday.

Mama touched his hand, which was resting on the

arm of her wheelchair. Her fingers felt hot and dry. They looked at each other silently for a long moment. "In time, you'll feel happier," she said at last. "Life often gets better all by itself."

Ned went to his room, thinking about the things grown-ups said to him. Would his mother ever get better all by herself? There were moments when he felt his parents' words were trying to steer him in a certain direction—Papa's more than Mama's—like the stick with which he had pushed paper boats across puddles.

It was nearly hot in the pew on Sunday. He was looking up at Papa as he preached but not listening closely. He was trying to imagine the delicious skunklike smell of dandelions and realizing you couldn't imagine a smell. He heard his father say, "And the blind and the lame came to him in the temple, and he healed them."

He thought of the Makepeace veranda filled with the blind and the lame; they crowded up against the doors and windows and climbed over the settee, and the cat with one eye slunk around their feet, trying to protect itself from being stepped upon. What if a fire started in one of those vast empty rooms he'd peered at through a window? And what if the fire raged along the hill and his own house was caught by it—sparks raining on the roof—flames licking up the boards of the attic floor and the long case that held the gun.

"Let us pray," said the Reverend Wallis. Ned bowed his head and shut his eyes tight and the fire went out.

"Could we visit Mr. Scully?" Ned asked his father on the way home.

"We'll do it today," Papa said. "It's been on my mind for a while. I'm glad you reminded me, Neddy."

The Waterville Nursing Home was a large brick building with two towers on the wide main street of town, not far from the store where Papa occasionally bought a box of homemade chocolates. Papa and Ned stood in a large central hall that smelled a little sour, like milk on the edge of turning. The floor was shiny and slippery with wax. On their right was a door that said OFFICE, and on the left was a huge room filled with chairs and tables. Three old women were sitting in it listening to a radio. One held an ear trumpet toward it which looked like a stag's antler. As Papa went to the office door it opened, and Mrs. Scallop glided out. She wore a white uniform and her hair was tied up in a bun. Everything about her looked different except for her smile, slow and triumphant, that seemed to say to Ned, "I am wonderful and I know secrets."

"Reverend Wallis, what brings you and darling Neddy here?"

"Why, Mrs. Scallop! How well you're looking!" exclaimed Papa. "We hoped to see Mr. Scully—if he's up to it and if you think it would be salutary."

She nodded and looked wise. "Salutary," she repeated. "Yes, indeed. He'll be glad to see you. He won't be able to say so. We're doing our best with him, Reverend, but there's been very little improvement."

She led them up a long staircase and down a narrow corridor past several closed doors until they came to Mr. Scully's room. His door was open. A pot of dead geraniums stood on the sill of the one window. Mrs. Scallop made clucking sounds as she walked to the other side of the bed, where the old man lay motionless on his side. "He loved his little pot of flowers," Mrs. Scallop said in a loud voice. "But I warned him geraniums don't do well in winter." She smiled widely and bent over the bed. "Guess who's here!"

Papa took Ned's hand firmly in his and walked around the foot of the bed to join Mrs. Scallop, and Ned felt his stomach sink the way it did when he turned over a rock and saw the sudden stirring of insects and worms.

Mr. Scully's hair was like fluff. There was a sparse

stubble of beard on his cheeks and chin. His lower lip looked frozen. But his eyes were bright with recognition and intelligence, and in that pale face which seemed made of ashes, they burned like coals. Ned leaned over him and whispered, "Hello, Mr. Scully. I'm glad to see you."

"Speak up, Neddy," commanded Mrs. Scallop.

"We hope our neighbor will come home soon," the Reverend Wallis said in a somewhat preaching voice. Ned found it extremely crowded there between the geranium and the narrow bed on which Mr. Scully lay. Just as he was thinking that, Papa and Mrs. Scallop moved out into the corridor and began speaking animatedly to each other.

Ned looked down at the old man, who moved one shoulder very slightly. Talking to someone who couldn't talk back to him was the strangest thing that had ever happened to Ned. He told Mr. Scully about his visits to the Makepeace mansion, and a little about school and what he was reading and learning. He didn't mention that he'd met Doris or that Mr. Scully's flivver had vanished or that the outhouse had been taken down. All at once, he ran out of words. Mr. Scully blinked. Ned thought he smiled very slightly, but he wasn't sure. Then, very slowly, the old man brought his hand out from under the white coverlet and made a brief, stroking gesture with it, as though he were patting an animal. Ned glanced up at Papa and Mrs. Scallop. They had moved further from the door. He leaned over the old man until his mouth was close to his ear. "I think I saw him," he whispered. "I'm pretty sure it was him at the edge of the woods, and he'd caught something to eat."

When he stood back, Mr. Scully's eyes were gleaming up at him.

While they were driving home, Ned asked his father if he could visit Mr. Scully again. Papa said he'd take him next Saturday when he was planning to do some research in the public library. "I'm sure it will do him good to see you, Ned," Papa said. "His daughter left rather abruptly for the West—I expect she had things she had to attend to—and now he's quite alone." He paused and seemed to hesitate. Then he said, "I feel that you ought to know he is not likely to get better."

"Do you mean that he's going to die?" Ned asked.

Papa's lips moved as though he were searching for a word.

"I know that," Ned said quickly. His father put his arm around his shoulders and hugged him.

Ned went to see Mama. He told her about visiting Mr. Scully. "Does Mrs. Scallop own the nursing home?" he asked.

"So that's how she looked!" exclaimed his mother,

and she started to laugh. He wasn't paying much attention to her—he was thinking of what he'd left out of the visit, his telling Mr. Scully about seeing the cat, or a cat.

"It's as I had imagined," Mama said. "She's happy now that she has her own kingdom."

Ned wasn't accustomed to feeling bored and restless when he was with Mama. But he was now, and he didn't want to talk about Mrs. Scallop and her kingdom anymore.

Papa had already started to prepare Sunday supper, and Ned went down to the kitchen. He usually enjoyed watching his father cook meals. Papa sprang from table to sink to stove like a deer. He seemed to Ned a different man from the one who had stood in Mr. Scully's room at the nursing home and spoken so stiffly to him. He picked up a potato in a fast, delicate way, like a raccoon picking up its food. He was telling Ned about an article he was preparing about the history of the church, of all the ministers who had preceded him there, some of whom were buried in the little graveyard near the parsonage. After a while, he got too busy to talk and Ned, to his surprise, found himself going up the back staircase, then up the attic stairs.

It was still daylight, and he didn't have to pull the

long string connected with the light bulb in the ceiling. He picked his way across the magazines and books and boxes and went to stand in the doorway of the unfinished room.

From where he stood, he could see the dust on the case that held the gun. He could hardly believe he had ever touched the case, that he'd taken out the gun and carried it down the stairs, past Mrs. Scallop sleeping in her bed, all the way to the hall and out the front door and down the overgrown road to the old stable.

He remembered how snugly the stock of the gun had fit against his shoulder. After a minute or two, he went to the small window and looked out. The sky was gray and luminous like the gray pearl stickpin Papa kept in a velvet box on his dresser top and which had belonged to Ned's grandfather. There was a breath of color among the tree branches, yellowish and rosy. Soon, Ned knew, lilies of the valley would push through the earth below the kitchen window and send out their perfume in blossoms that were like small bells. Soon it would be Easter vacation, though there was still snow on the ground.

There would be an Easter egg hunt on the lawn near the parsonage for the Sunday school children. On Easter Sunday, his mother would be carried down to the Packard, driven to church and carried to the pew where she and Ned would listen to Papa's Easter sermon. He would be sitting there next to her, pretending as he always did when she was brought to church, that she could stand up and walk like everyone else.

Papa spent three more Saturday afternoons at the library in Waterville, and on those days, he dropped Ned off at the nursing home so he could· visit Mr. Scully. Mr. Scully, Ned realized, was the only person he really wanted to see.

He got used to the froggy, sour smell of the wax but he didn't get used to Mrs. Scallop in her uniform with her new tightly bound hair.

Although she smiled all the time, she still had her old ways. On his first visit alone, she asked Ned, "Now, what interesting thing have you to tell me?"

"They're almost finished building the new garage near school," he offered.

Still smiling, Mrs. Scallop said, "Are you being insulting, Neddy dear?"

He worried suddenly that she might not let him up the stairs to see Mr. Scully. He tried to think of something that would interest her. She took hold of his arm and held it tightly. "Go along! You can find your own way. Mrs. Scallop understands boys, young or old!"

As he went up the stairs, he thought of something he was sure would have interested her—how he had crept by her room one night months ago, carrying a Daisy rifle. It made him smile to himself to think of telling her, but in an unpleasant, grim way. He was pretty sure that it had not been Mrs. Scallop looking out the window when he came home that night. He had begun to doubt that there had been anyone watching him.

A tall woman in a nurse's uniform was standing next to Mr. Scully's bed, holding his wrist in her hand. She looked at Ned and smiled and said, "You must be Mr. Scully's friend."

Ned nodded. "I'm nurse Clay," she said. She lowered Mr. Scully's wrist gently and pulled the cover up over his shoulder. "He'll be pleased to see you," she said as she left the room.

How still Mr. Scully was! Did something inside him run about—trying to find a way out? What did he think about?

Ned recalled the joke he had played years ago on a night when Papa had come to hear him say his prayer: *Now I lay me down to sleep, I pray the Lord my soul to keep* . . . Ned had put a pillow beneath his blanket and then he had crawled beneath his bed.

Papa had spoken to the pillow for a long time and Ned choked up with laughter. Papa had laughed, too, when Ned grabbed hold of one of his ankles and emerged from beneath the bed. It must have happened before Mama got sick; Papa had laughed so much in those days. He had imitated Cosmo, Mama's horse, and galloped through the long living room. And he had made jokes that were almost as funny as Mama's jokes. Those were the days when he did everything as quickly as he made supper, and those were the days, too, when his voice nearly always sounded real.

Ned walked around to the other side of the bed and said softly, "Hello, Mr. Scully." He waited for a minute until he recalled that the old man couldn't answer with a greeting of his own. He stared up at Ned, his eyes bright and alive as they'd been last time. But he looked faintly changed—as though he'd sunk further into the bed somehow.

"Someone has cleaned up your yard," Ned told him. "I stop by there every day after school."

Mr. Scully blinked.

"I was pretty sure the cat was dead," Ned said, lowering his voice.

Mr. Scully moved his head, which made the pillow whisper. His mouth opened slightly.

"He never came back to the shed. But now I'm pretty sure that cat I saw was him. Maybe he had a mouse in his mouth. Maybe he's learned to hunt even with one eye."

The old man was looking over his shoulder. Ned felt hollow. He turned to see what Mr. Scully was staring at. There was only the plant on the windowsill, brown and dusty, the earth dry around it.

"Do you want me to take the plant away?" Ned asked.

Mr. Scully moaned and blinked his eyes.

"It might make Mrs. Scallop get into a temper," he said. Mr. Scully squeezed his eyes the way people do when they smile. "Maybe she won't get mad at you," Ned said, hoping Mr. Scully was trying to smile, "because you can't talk back."

The hollow feeling which had gone away came back. Ned began to speak about school and what he was studying and how hard arithmetic was, and his voice sounded to himself exactly the way it did when he was answering questions Miss Brewster or other grown-ups asked him. He surprised himself by breaking off in the middle of all the school talk and describing instead the stone house at the corner of the dirt road, and the long veranda of the Makepeace mansion, and how he felt there by himself, looking out over the whole countryside. He felt better, filled up with interest. But there came a moment when he grew tired of his own solitary voice, when the little room seemed to hold silence and nothing else. He told Mr. Scully goodbye and promised to come back and see him again, and he took the plant with him out into the hall, not sure what he would do with it. Nurse Clay emerged suddenly from another room and he held it out to her wordlessly. "I've been meaning to take that away," she said. "I'll try and find a living plant for Mr. Scully."

He went downstairs and out the front doors of the nursing home without running into Mrs. Scallop. That was lucky, he thought, still hearing the echoes of his own voice the way he'd heard them as he spoke in Mr. Scully's room. When he found Papa in the library, he asked him, "Do you ever feel peculiar when you're preaching and you suddenly hear yourself and there's no one answering you?"

Papa looked at him thoughtfully for a moment. "Sometimes," he said. "Most of the time, I feel all the people in the congregation are talking with me, inside their hearts, perhaps."

Ned could see it was different for Papa than it was for him when he spoke to Mr. Scully, although now that he thought of it, he might have sounded a bit preachy when he was speaking to the old man about school and all that.

Mr. Scully was weaker, it seemed to Ned, the next Saturday he saw him. He didn't blink once, just stared at Ned, his eyes half-closed. Nurse Clay told him to speak very softly and that his visit must be brief. He hardly said anything during the few minutes he stood beside Mr. Scully's bed. He felt an impulse to touch him, his shoulder, his white cheek, but he was afraid that it would startle the old man, or that his skin would feel as fragile and dusty as a moth's wing.

Mrs. Scallop caught him just as he was going out the doors. She held his arm and shook her head sorrowfully.

"We won't have Mr. Scully with us much longer, I fear," she said. She drew him quickly into her arms, and as he pulled away from her, she announced to the ceiling that the Lord worked in mysterious ways. He didn't see how those words—which he'd heard many times before in church—were applicable to Mr. Scully, but they certainly were to Mrs. Scallop.

When he arrived the following Saturday, Nurse Clay and Mrs. Scallop were talking in the hall. The old lady with the ear trumpet like a stag's antler was creeping slowly down the steps. Nurse Clay told him he couldn't visit for more than five minutes today. And Mrs. Scallop, her nostrils flaring, said, "Do exactly as Nurse Clay says. No shilly-shallying this time."

Ned's anger at Mrs. Scallop's unfairness blotted out what Nurse Clay had said, but he recalled her words when he was standing next to Mr. Scully's bed. The shade was drawn, the old man's eyes were shut. By listening hard, Ned caught a faint sound of slow breathing, each breath like a sigh.

"Mr. Scully?" he whispered.

Mr. Scully's eyes fluttered open. He looked blind, then very slowly his eyes focused on Ned.

"I know you're not feeling well, so I won't stay long," Ned said. He felt dizzy; Mr. Scully seemed to be looking straight into the center of him.

"Oh, Mr. Scully . . ." Ned said, wishing desperately that he was somewhere else, that he hadn't come. Something was hurrying him, urging him toward he didn't know what. He heard his own loud breathing. The old man lay still, imprisoned in his mysterious affliction. Was he the very same man who had stood next to Ned at the kitchen sink and leaned forward so eagerly to watch the cat playing with a leaf?

"Oh, Mr. Scully—" Ned said again. "It was me that shot the cat."

He wanted to cram his words back inside himself. From far off, he heard and recognized the sound of tables being set for a meal, the clink of flatware and dishes, the rattle of trays. An elderly man in a bathrobe went slowly past Mr. Scully's door, his head thrust forward, stiffly held, as though he were watching out for dangers that might lie in his path. Inside the room, there was no sound now. Ned couldn't hear Mr. Scully's breathing. He felt utterly alone. He saw, in his mind's eye, the tail of the animal which had moved so quickly along the foundation of the stable, its shadow larger and looser than it, like water flowing, and the shadows of weeds cast by moonlight against the stones, all magnified in this instant as though his memory had become a microscope directed toward that moment when he'd held the Daisy, and its power seemed to be growing and becoming ever sharper, ever clearer. He felt his finger tighten as though he were pulling back on a trigger. He gasped and looked down.

Mr. Scully had moved his head and Ned could see a little of his other cheek, quilted with wrinkles. He was looking straight at Ned. His mouth moved. Then his hand began a hesitant, inching journey toward Ned's hand, which rested on the coverlet.

Nurse Clay appeared in the doorway. "I think that's all for today, Ned," she said softly.

Ned didn't move. He couldn't, watching that hand labor toward his.

"Ned?" the nurse called.

He felt the touch of Mr. Scully's finger, then gradually his whole hand covering Ned's own. There was the faintest pressure, so faint, Ned wasn't sure how he knew there'd been any at all.

Mr. Scully's head fell back against the pillow, his eyes closed, the hand which had pressed Ned's fluttered and lay still upon the cover. Ned went out of the room, passing Nurse Clay on her way in. He heard a groan and glanced back. Nurse Clay was leaning over the slight body on the bed, hiding it from view.

Ned walked to the library. He raised the hand Mr. Scully had touched and looked at it as though it could talk. Finally, he had spoken to another person about shooting the cat. Mr. Scully had been unable to speak. Yet he had pressed that hand. He wouldn't have done that if he had thought Ned was truly bad. But he must have had a thought about Ned. Still, he'd tried to comfort him. He had understood that Ned was suffering. What *would* he have said? He hadn't ever had to lie to Mr. Scully the way he had at home— except by leaving out a few things he knew about that cat. Mr. Scully was going to die; he was leaving

Ned perched on the top rung of a ladder built out of lies; the ladder was leaning against nothing.

In the library, Papa looked up at Ned from the oak table on which several books lay open.

"Ned? Are you feeling ill?" he asked with concern.

Ned saw two lines on either side of Papa's mouth; he didn't think he'd noticed how deep they were before. Someone shook out a newspaper at another table. If he went to the window near the librarian's desk, he would be able to look down at the street that ran alongside the river. He had always loved going to that street full of the smells of river water and oil. Once, when he and Papa had been walking along there, maybe to buy new shoes, or go to the barbershop, and he'd been holding Papa's hand and watching his own feet move along the sidewalk, he'd let go for a moment or so, then he had reached up and taken hold of the hand again. But when he'd looked up to say something to Papa, it was another man's hand he'd been holding onto. The stranger was smiling and Ned had looked back along the street and seen Papa standing near the barbershop and laughing. Everyone who had seen what Ned had done had laughed, and finally he had, too, and he loved the street for that as well as for its watery, oily smells, because he felt safe there, a place where he could take anyone's hand, and where everyone seemed to know him.

Papa asked, "Is Mr. Scully worse?"

Ned nodded. He felt his eyes fill. Papa took a large white handkerchief from his breast pocket and held it out to him. Ned wiped his tears away, and Papa got up and put his arm around Ned's shoulders, then gathered his books to return them to the librarian. They paused on the library steps. The March wind brought them the smell of the river, which, today, smelled more of Easter lilies than it did of oil. The sky was pale where it showed through the ragged clouds. Ned recollected suddenly the gypsies they had seen last October, the harsh, strong colors of their clothes. He wished he could see them right now, their dark, vivid faces so indifferent to everything around them as though it were all a dream they drove their caravans through.

When they were seated in the Packard, Papa said, "I think it was not wise of me to let you visit Mr. Scully. I knew he'd been failing. Try to remember, Ned, that he is a very old man, that he's had a long, long life."

The car was rumbling and Ned wished they'd drive away.

"I'm proud of you, Ned," Papa said. "I'm proud of your concern for David Scully."

Ned sank deep into the plush of the seat.

"You will discover yourself as you get older that people don't behave as they should. Doris has not been the best of daughters. She did her duty only in a grudging way. Your visits to him have been very important. I know they lightened his heart."

Ned was suddenly so angry he wanted to howl—"It's because of the cat I went to see him!"

Yet that wasn't true! It was just a piece of the truth.

A church deacon had given him a toy safe years ago. He'd lost the safe and its key but he remembered, out of a number of secret things he put there, one of the tiny glasses which held communion wine and which he'd slipped into his pocket one Sunday when no one was watching, and which he liked to drink water from, a chipped stone he'd found which he was sure was an Indian arrowhead, and a note he'd written when he first learned how to print which said: "What is a holy ghost?"

Mr. Scully had now become his safe, holding a larger secret than he'd ever had before.

More than the secret of the cat had drawn him to the nursing home. It was Mr. Scully himself. He'd known *him*, his habits, the things he knew how to do, the way he made his bread, the way he could get a fire started so quickly in the stove, the stories he told, the smile he gave Ned when he poured rum into his own tea, his memories of his long life.

He glanced at Papa. "I once stole a communion glass," he said.

Papa said, "Oh, yes. When you were little. I remember I saw you drinking water from it one night in the bathroom."

"Why didn't you say anything?"

Papa grinned suddenly. "Well—if you'd done it again, I might have."

Evelyn opened the front door to them. Behind her stood Mrs. Kimball wearing her brown silk Sunday dress with its small lace collar. Ned had once seen her remove the collar as though it had been a necklace and place it between two pieces of tissue paper and put it away in a drawer of the dresser which stood in her kitchen.

"What is it?" Papa asked at once.

"Mrs. Wallis has been in awful pain," Mrs. Kimball replied. "I've made her as comfortable as I could, Reverend."

Ned could feel Evelyn watching him closely.

Papa was running upstairs.

"Ned, I've left a pot of soup for your supper on the stove. When Evie came by, I sent her back home to get a loaf of fresh bread for you."

"Your Ma was crying without making any noise," Evelyn said to him, her eyes wide.

"Evie!" exclaimed Mrs. Kimball. "Can't you see how worried Ned is? Let him go to her!"

Ned ran up the stairs and across the landing where the stained-glass window spilled its colors, grape and lemon and raspberry, upon the oak floor. He halted beside the pier glass which was as dark as a well at this time of day. Papa was carrying Mama from her wheelchair to her bed. She was pressed against him, her arms and legs drawn close as though she were knotted. Ned watched, breathless, as Papa lowered her onto the bed, glanced blankly into the hall and shut the door.

He went out of the house and ran down to the furthest edge of the field closest to the monastery. He sat on a stone that had come loose from the old dividing wall. Around him, the bony leafless branches of the sumac rattled in the wind. Once he heard a bell ring distantly.

At last lights went on in the living room. From where he was sitting and waiting, the house looked like a distant ship. He felt he could go home now. Mama must be better, or else asleep, if Papa was downstairs. From all the times before when Mama had gotten so sick, Ned knew Papa wouldn't leave her until she was all right.

When Ned walked into the hall, Papa, his face strained and exhausted, was staring at a letter on the table next to the coat stand. "I haven't opened the mail," he said to Ned in a distracted voice. Ned stared at him mutely. Papa suddenly smiled and seemed to see Ned all at once as though he'd waked up out of a doze.

"She is better, Neddy. It's the dampness this time of year. It's so hard on her, and this old house . . . it can be so chilly. She's awake. You can visit her. I believe Mrs. Kimball mentioned soup . . ." Papa walked rather dreamily in the direction of the kitchen.

"Papa," Ned called. "You forgot to take off your coat!" His father looked down at himself. "You're right. I've had it on all this time."

Ned didn't wait to see Papa hang up his coat but went straight up to his mother's room. She was leaning back against several pillows.

"Ned," she said gently, "don't look so scared. I'm much better. You know how it's always been with this sickness. But there's hopeful news, I think. Papa has been reading about a new treatment. He's already spoken to Dr. Nevins about it. It has something to do with gold salts, injecting them, and they can reduce the inflammation. That's what hurts, you see."

"Does it hurt now?"

"It's not bad," she said. He knew that meant the pain hadn't gone away.

Papa came to the door holding a letter. "Now look where Hilary has got to," he said. "The Territory of Hawaii!" He put the letter down on the bed and said he had to get back to the kitchen and heat up Mrs. Kimball's soup for everyone's supper.

"You can open the letter, Ned," Mama told him.

He drew three sheets of paper from the envelope. On one was a drawing below a note addressed to him. He held out the other pages to Mama. She didn't reach for them but kept her hands beneath the blanket. "I can't hold anything yet," she said.

The drawing was of a ship. Ned had never seen one like it. The note read:

Dear Ned,

Here is a Chinese junk, and look how high the deck is! It's very much like a 16th century merchantman. The sails of most junks are brilliant red. It's beautiful, like a glorious insect, and I'm going to sail the China seas on one like this. Wish you were with me!

Ned held up the drawing so Mama could see it. "I'd love to see that sailing up the river," she said. "It would rouse up the ghost of Henry Hudson."

She smiled at him. It was a calm smile yet it had a kind of tightness in it, an effort, so Ned knew he'd better go. He picked up Uncle Hilary's letter and said he'd take it down to Papa, and she thanked him and said she might sleep a little now.

After Papa had read the letter, he told Ned that Uncle Hilary was going to visit a leper colony at Molokai where a priest, Father Damien, had gone to live to minister to the lepers. Afterwards, Uncle Hilary was going to Hong Kong to find a junk he could sail on.

Ned and Papa ate Mrs. Kimball's soup, which was not very tasty but quite filling. For once, Ned wasn't so interested in Uncle Hilary's whereabouts and doings. He had homework to do for Monday but what he was thinking about mostly was sickness, his mother's and Mr. Scully's. He didn't want a colony of lepers on his mind, too.

"What is your sermon about tomorrow, Papa?" Ned asked, trying to think of a way he might be able to get out of going to church.

"The text is from Paul's letter to the Philippians: 'Do all things without grumbling or questioning that you may be blameless and innocent—' " Ned's father suddenly broke off and reached across the table and took Ned's hand in his. "As you do them, my Ned," he said. "Dear Ned."

He nearly told Papa then—he felt about to burst with all that he'd hidden. He could feel everything pressing against his closed mouth as he stared up at the camel in its glass desert on the Tiffany shade. But he said nothing, and pretty soon Papa got up and began to clear away the dishes. Ned could hear him in the kitchen, fixing a tray for Mama. He was whistling the way he sometimes did after an especially hard day.

Dr. Nevins came on Wednesday of the following week and began Mama's treatment, which was called chrysotherapy. The only thing she minded about it, she told Ned later, was that she couldn't sit near the bay windows for a while because any exposure to light after you'd been given gold salts could turn your skin blue. And the salts made your mouth itch.

"But never mind all that!" she said. "Look!"

She had put her hands flat down on her tray and straightened her fingers. "I feel like silk, Neddy. I might even be able to walk into church on Easter Sunday. Think of the effect on the choir! They might be shocked into perfect harmony!"

It astonished him to see her so happy. He hadn't ever thought of her as really unhappy except, of course, when she was in severe pain, but she had sometimes seemed to him like a person watching a parade from a distance, making comments, some serious, some joking, about the marchers. As he looked at her face now, her eyes so wide and her mouth smiling, it was as if she'd flung herself right into the middle of the parade and wasn't a watcher anymore. It frightened him a little.

Her glance steady on him, she took his hand in hers. He felt the grip of her fingers, the unfevered warmth. "Ned, Ned . . ." she murmured. "Take the good when it comes. We must try to not be scared."

Because of trying to be not scared, he told Papa on Saturday that he would like to visit Mr. Scully even if he could only spend a minute with him.

"Are you sure, Ned?" Papa asked. "You were unhappy last week after you'd seen him. Let me telephone Mrs. Scallop when we get home, and if he is better, I'll take you to see him after school next week."

Ned felt that if he didn't see Mr. Scully today, he wouldn't have enough nerve to last him all the way to some afternoon next week. He had a sudden vision of Mr. Scully so small that he wouldn't make a wrinkle in the nursing home cot's worn white cover. But all he told Papa was that he was sure Mr. Scully expected him. Papa dropped him off in front of the nursing home before driving on to the library.

The large hall was empty. In the patients' living room, he saw Mrs. Scallop straightening an old woman's sleeve, pulling it tight and buttoning it around her wrist. When she noticed Ned, she didn't take a step toward him or smile, or even frown. He felt invisible and uncertain. Should he go upstairs?

"Ned?" It was Nurse Clay speaking to him. She was in the doorway of the office. She beckoned to him. When he was standing in front of her, she touched his hair.

"Your old friend has gone," she said softly.

He looked at her, not comprehending her words.

"Mr. Scully died in his sleep," she said. "It was on Monday."

Ned was very still for a moment. He felt his own stillness as a kind of sleep where he was safe. Then he burst out of it. "Did it hurt him to die?" he asked.

Nurse Clay said, "I think it didn't."

Mrs. Scallop had come into the hall, and he saw her look quickly and measuringly from himself to Nurse Clay. Her face then assumed a mournful look.

"Poor Ned. I know how you must feel."

He knew why she hadn't made any sign of recognition to him when he'd arrived. She had been waiting for Nurse Clay to tell him about Mr. Scully's death. He realized all at once that Mrs. Scallop was not simply a silly, unpredictable person but a scared one. She had been scared to tell him what had happened.

Nurse Clay then told Ned that there had been a simple funeral on Thursday, attended by a distant cousin of Mr. Scully's. All the time she was speaking, Mrs. Scallop stood there, her hands gripped over her stomach, staring intently at Ned.

When Nurse Clay had gone upstairs to take care of patients—perhaps, Ned thought, of someone who was now in Mr. Scully's former room—Mrs. Scallop said, "I hope you'll come and see us even though your only reason for visiting was Mr. Scully."

"I have to go," Ned said, not looking at her.

"I see you have no tears for the old man," Mrs. Scallop observed. "Sensible boy! There's no use in crying for folks when they've passed on."

He didn't know what to say to her. All the sadness he had felt for Mr. Scully had filled him in that first moment he'd seen him lying on the floor with his arms outstretched. All along Ned had been expecting Mr. Scully to die. There was no point in explaining that to Mrs. Scallop. She was a person to whom nothing, he thought, could ever be explained. She was locked inside of her own opinions like a prisoner. He said goodbye to her, caught a faintly bewildered look on her face, and fled out the doors to the street.

"They might have telephoned me for your sake," Papa said when Ned had told him of Mr. Scully's death. "Mrs. Scallop certainly knew you were concerned."

There was nothing more to be said about Mrs. Scallop.

"He fixed up all his things," Ned said to Papa. "He went through all the boxes and satchels in his attic."

"I never knew him as well as you did, Neddy," Papa said. "He always kept to himself and didn't seem to want company."

It was true, Ned thought. Mr. Scully had been *his* friend. As they drove past the little old house and then turned right, up the Wallis driveway, Ned was comforted by that knowledge. Together, he and Mr. Scully had taken care of the wounded animal, and in the end, Ned had told Mr. Scully what he had done. He would never know now what the pressure of Mr. Scully's hand on his own had meant.

He sighed aloud as he tried to imagine what the old man would have said if he'd been able to speak. "A boy would do that," Mr. Scully had remarked the

201

first time they'd seen the cat through the kitchen window.

Ned strained to recall how Mr. Scully's voice had sounded that day. It hadn't been an angry or especially disappointed tone of voice, Ned was pretty sure, but more the way anyone might speak about Hudson Valley weather, something that wasn't always pleasant but nothing you could change by complaining about it.

Mr. Scully's house was covered with workmen the next week; they seemed to be shaking the last of the old man's presence from it. Men threw down the rotted shingles from the roof and painted the clapboard and extended the roof of the woodshed so that it looked big enough to shelter a car. Ned saw Mr. Kimball working on the kitchen window frame.

The new gasoline station down near school on the state road was completed, and Mr. Kimball got steady work there, only doing carpentry to bring in extra money, Evelyn explained to Ned when she showed him her new shoes. She fussed about them all the way home because the ground was damp and spongy with spring rains.

The big news among the four children was that Billy would be moving to Albany in May. His father had gotten a job there with a plumbing contractor.

Times were getting better, but you still had to grab a chance when it was offered, Billy quoted his father as saying. For the first time, he mentioned his brother who had infantile paralysis and needed special care which cost a terrible lot of money. Ned was sorry that Billy was going North. They had begun to be friends.

Everyone seemed to be disappearing. Mr. Scully was dead. Billy was moving away. Uncle Hilary was sailing in a Chinese junk somewhere on the China seas. Even Evelyn was disappearing in a way, becoming a different Evelyn, her hair brushed neatly, her feet in new shoes, her smile a little prissy as though she were trying on a grown-up face.

One night in the middle of April, a few days before Easter, Ned woke to hear the boards creaking outside his door. He got up and tiptoed out into the hall and stood still and listened. He heard footsteps on the stairs. It was nearly pitch-dark but he could make out the flutter of something white going down to the central hall. He leaned on the bannister, knowing it was Mama. He didn't call out to her. He thought she might like to walk about alone, the way he always had, feeling the freedom in the silence and darkness.

It was strange to think of the two of them, awake, yet not speaking, both of them up in the middle of the night. The monks would be asleep in their monastery until matins summoned them to pray. And Sport would be curled up in his doghouse. All the Kimball babies would be sleeping in their rattling old cribs that had been passed on from one Kimball child to the next.

But there would be creatures stirring in the woods. Owls would be hunting small prey. And the wild cats might be on the prowl in the pine woods north of the old stable or at the edge of the Makepeace property. And the earth itself, beginning to be warm now, would be full of creeping and crawling living things.

For the first time in many weeks, Ned thought of the gun in the attic. A great longing came over him to go up there, to look at it. Papa had said he could have it, perhaps in a year or two. It was his gun.

A shudder went through him; it was so violent, he held on to the bannister as though to keep himself from falling. Papa had said another thing. There was nothing to imagine with a gun except something that was dead.

He let go of the bannister and went quickly to his room where he threw on clothes right over his pajamas. The only thing he could think of was to get out of the house, get as far from the attic as he could.

When he was dressed, carrying his shoes in his hand, he went to the head of the stairs and listened. He could hear nothing. Mama must still be up, or else he would have heard her return to her room. Perhaps she was in the kitchen making herself a cup of tea.

He didn't even consider how strange an idea that was, that his mother should be able to do such a thing for herself. All he thought about as he went softly down the stairs and through the hall and opened the front door as quietly as he could was that he must get away.

Once he was outside, he didn't seem to have to make up his mind which way to go. It was as though he were being led. He went due south, to the maple woods, then through them until he was on the other side, looking up at the moon-white columns of the Makepeace mansion.

VIII

Cat's Moon

NED SHIVERED. HE WAS WEARING A SWEATER AND HIS dark blue school knickers, but he hadn't bothered to pull on stockings, just slipped his feet into his shoes, and around his bare ankles he felt the dampness of a ground mist which hung over the long meadow like a sheet of thin smoke. The moon was nearly full. Its light glinted on the water of the river. As a sickle cuts away tall grass, the moonlight had cut away a great swath of the dark, and raggle-taggle edges of light lay upon the boards of the veranda.

He went to sit on the old settee. He put his arm along its rounded headrest, feeling through his sweater the rough tips of twigs which had worked free, and he leaned back until his head was resting against the wall. The clapboard was dry, slightly warm, as though the sun had shone upon it all day. As he began to see better in the dark, he could make out individual trees in the mass of woods to the south. Where moonlight cast their shadows on the ground, he saw white puffs like smoke, perhaps the petals of blood-root or early everlasting.

Now he was calm. His thoughts were quiet and fleeting and wordless. He could smell the new wild grass and wildflowers and the strong black odor of earth. He glimpsed the port and starboard lights of a boat southward bound on the Hudson, and he imagined himself standing on the deck, looking down on the kite tails of moonlight on the water. He got up and walked along the veranda. The old house shifted, the boards he stepped upon creaked. A breeze started up from the north and swept across the meadow, clearing away the mist and, like a single breath taken and expelled, it rustled and was gone. Home seemed far away and the gun in the attic weightless as a shadow. He turned back. Someone was coming toward him from the border of maple trees. He held his breath for an instant.

The figure stepped up onto the veranda and raised one arm.

"Neddy?"

"Mama," he said.

She was wrapped up in her old tweed coat that fell nearly to her ankles. They sat down together on the settee.

"In India—when you can't sleep—they say it's because there's a cat's moon," she said in a low voice.

"Every time I shut my eyes, I got more wide awake," he said.

"Just now when we were standing next to each other, I realized you've grown as tall as I am," she said. "Did you notice that?"

He hadn't noticed it. What seemed strange was not to be looking down at her, not to be looking mostly at her hair and forehead.

"Is it all right for you to be out walking around like this?" he asked.

"I think it is," she said. "Even if it weren't, I think I would have to—it is marvelous. . ."

"Will that medicine cure your sickness?"

"It has given me a vacation. The doctor isn't sure how it works. We'll have to see."

They were speaking in very low voices as seemed right in the night's softness.

"I think there's bloodroot growing down there," he said.

208

"You remembered the name of it!"

"And early everlasting," he said. "And trillium maybe."

She remarked that the names alone were so lovely, one needn't see the flowers.

"You'll be able to walk into church on Easter Sunday," he said.

"Oh, yes. I hope so."

"Maybe the Makepeace family used to sit out here like we are," he said.

"Perhaps they did. Spring wakes people up. The girls and their young brothers might have run around the meadow on a night like this. It makes you want to run—this air."

"Then they went off to war," Ned said. "And the Germans shot them."

"They went off to war with guns and other men shot them," she said. She touched his arm. "Do you think we're too heavy for this old thing?" she asked. "I heard a distinct crack."

They stood up and began to walk side by side.

"I miss Mr. Scully," Ned said.

She was silent a moment. They were passing a huge dark window. She paused and leaned her forehead against it and peered inside.

"Nobody there . . ." she murmured. She took his

arm for a moment. "We must all part, Ned," she said.

The meaning of what she had said to him so quietly—almost shyly—came to him slowly as sleep sometimes did: I am falling asleep, he would say to himself, but not yet, not yet, and then he would. So now he said to himself, I understand what she said— we must all part, we must, we must—and at that moment, as the sorrow of it seemed to lodge in his throat so that it was hard to breathe, a cat walked straight out of the woods and into the moonlight.

"Look!" he whispered.

A second cat, smaller than the first, followed it. The first cat stood straight up on its hind feet, and the second made a wreath around it. They leaped, they tumbled, they jumped and pounced, into patches of darkness then back into the light.

"They're dancing," Mama breathed.

Ned stepped upon the ground from the edge of the veranda and walked a few feet down the slope of the meadow. The first cat cocked its head and looked in Ned's direction, but the other, smaller animal, ran back into the shelter of the woods.

"Mama! There are two kittens. I can see them, just there by the silver spruce."

He heard her low laugh. "How lovely!" she said.

210

"It's a cat family out for a walk. It really is a cat's moon."

The dark small shapes of the kittens rolled each other up like snowballs and vanished. Now only the first cat remained. Ned crouched, the better to see. The cat looked directly at him. He saw the empty socket where its eye had been. Suddenly, as though that second was all the cat would allow Ned, it moved swiftly away and vanished, too.

"We must go home," Mama called. "The wind is rising . . . We'll catch colds."

He stood up and turned back to the mansion. The moon was behind it and its shadow fell like a mantle upon the ground before it.

His mother had stepped off the veranda and was looking up at the house, too. She recited something as if only to herself.

"The cloud-capp'd towers, the gorgeous palaces,
The solemn temples, the great globe itself . . ."

"Is that from the Bible?" Ned asked.

"No, it's William Shakespeare—from a play called *The Tempest.*"

They walked to the file of maple trees. The moon would be setting any minute. It had grown much

211

darker. She took his arm as they stepped over the long-ago collapsed stone wall and emerged on Wallis land.

"That cat had only one eye," he said quickly to her. "I shot it, and that's why."

She halted. She said his name once, inquiringly, as though she was not sure he'd spoken.

"After Papa put the gun away when Uncle Hilary gave it to me, I went up to the attic and got it. I went to the stable, and I saw something move. I aimed at it and shot. A cat turned up at Mr. Scully's with one eye. We fed it and took care of it. It almost died and then it got better. Then Mr. Scully got sick. And I kept feeding the cat. But it stopped coming to Mr. Scully's woodshed. One time I saw it at the Makepeace place—where we saw it tonight."

The silence around them was immense. He imagined that all the creatures sliding and creeping and walking about in the dark were listening to him. He couldn't see his mother's face. She was so still, like a tree standing there.

"It was the same cat we saw just now. The one that came to Mr. Scully's. A one-eyed cat."

"Someone else, something else, might have hurt it," she said. "You don't know for sure."

He thought for a moment. Then he said, "Maybe. But I shot something. I knew it was alive. When I

212

aimed the gun at whatever was moving, I didn't care, Mama." He heard, and was surprised, at how loud and sure his voice was. She reached out and took his hand and pulled him a little—he felt rooted to the spot. Then he gripped her fingers and they went on toward the house. When they came to the maple tree from whose branch he liked to swing out over the bank, over her old rock garden, she paused again.

"I saw you that night," she said. "I had gotten up, and it was one of those times I could walk. I was happy whenever that happened. I heard you going to the attic, then out the front door. After a time I tracked you. I went to the attic, too. I sat for a bit in that old Morris chair. Then I looked out a window and saw you coming back to the house, carrying something."

"It *was* you," he said. "It was the gun I was carrying. I thought that face at the window was Mrs. Scallop's. After a while, I began to think I just made it up, or dreamed that someone had seen me."

They were close to the porch. He could make out the steps and the shape of the lilac which would bloom in another month, he knew, and then the great purple blossoms would fill the hall with their scent.

"All this time you've had it on your mind," she said. "Since September."

"I told Mr. Scully but he couldn't speak anymore.

He couldn't move. I know he heard me, though. I don't know what he thought."

"Maybe he knew already," she said. "Let's sit on the steps a moment. I feel out of breath."

He sat down next to her, holding his chin in one hand. He felt the comfort of his own house behind him. When he sat on the Makepeace veranda, it was as if he'd gone to another country. He glanced at his mother. He wasn't waiting for anything to happen now; he wasn't waiting to say anything to her.

"I want to tell you something about myself," she said. "I ran away from home when you were three years old. I went north, to Maine. I found a cottage on a river and lived in it for about three months. It was a tidal river, and the tides dropped around ten feet. At night, I could hear the water gurgling. I remember it sounded like several very large people in a bathtub."

He laughed a little. It didn't stop him from being afraid of what she was telling him.

"I bought a rusty old bicycle and rode to the village nearby every day, where I got my groceries. I bought jam and bread and cider and sometimes, apples. I ate like a child eats. And I went to the library once a week. It was so quiet where I was except for the river. I used to get up at dawn. Herons and egrets would be feeding in the mud."

He heard in her voice how much she had liked it there.

"Why did you run away?" he asked.

She said, "I was afraid of your father's goodness. I'm not so very good."

He could not understand that. But he couldn't remember that she'd ever been gone, either. It was as though he'd been suddenly let into a room where only grown-up people live and talk, and he couldn't understand the language yet. But something stirred in his mind, in his memory, a kind of feeling of familiarity, of hearing something that—even if he didn't understand it—he had heard before.

"Why did you come back?" he asked softly.

"Papa and I wrote to each other. He didn't tell me right away about you walking all over the house at night. Yes . . . that's what you used to do. You found your way everywhere, little as you were, and because you were up all night, you were sleepy all day. I came back because I missed you both so much. And I came back so you would stop that night-walking and get a night's sleep."

He could tell by her voice that she was making a joke. She often made jokes when she was sad. He knew that just as he knew that Papa whistled when times were hard.

She was silent for a little while.

"Do you think you knew it was a cat—that night?" she asked finally.

"No. I knew it was *something*. I pretended it was a shadow. Then I got so I didn't know whether I was pretending or not."

He was thinking about her being so far away and how he had gone up and down the stairs in the house at night those months she was away, into all the rooms, probably up to the attic, too.

"This time it was you who came looking for me," he said.

"Yes. I saw you walking toward the maples. I followed you."

The doors behind them opened and light shone on them. They both stood up and turned.

Papa was standing in the doorway, the hall light on. He was wearing his bathrobe and his worn leather slippers.

He shaded his eyes with one hand and peered out at them.

"There you are!" he said. He smiled. "I've been looking all over the house for you. Then I thought— they've gone for a walk on this beautiful spring night."

"We went to the Makepeace mansion," Mama said.

"I'm so glad you've come home," Papa said.